3301329219

CW00368908

Long Ride into Hell

When Hugo Lyedekker, along with other fugitives from the Yuma Territorial Prison, held up a passenger train in Arizona he hadn't realized he was about to hit the jackpot. For aboard that train were a number of high-level VIPs including the Attorney-General, senators and Supreme Court Judges.

Seeing his chance to demand a large ransom and a pardon, Lyedekker sends word to the President himself in Washington. But this proves to be his first mistake for Frank Angel is given the mission to bring back the hostages alive – by whatever means necessary and with no questions asked!

Before long, the Maricopas mountains will run red with blood. . . .

By the same author

Standoff at Liberty
Ride Out to Vengeance
Ambush in Purgatory

Long Ride into Hell

Daniel Rockfern

A Black Horse Western

ROBERT HALE · LONDON

© Frederick Nolan 2005
First published in Great Britain 2005

ISBN 0 7090 7643 6

Robert Hale Limited
Clerkenwell House
Clerkenwell Green
London EC1R 0HT

Typeset by
Derek Doyle & Associates, Shaw Heath.
Printed and bound in Great Britain by
Antony Rowe Limited, Wiltshire.

1

By the time Angel reached the Attorney-General's office he was good and mad. His annoyance had been brought on by the total refusal of everyone he'd been in contact with to tell him just what was going on.

The surest way to rouse Angel's anger was to keep him in the dark. To treat him like an idiot. The trouble was, that just happened to be the way things were turning out. And Angel didn't like it.

Not one little bit.

He was ready to express his feelings in no uncertain terms to whoever it was sitting behind the Old Man's desk during the Attorney-General's absence, and who appeared to be creating wholesale chaos.

Angel strode into the outer office full of frustrated rage. The sight of Amabel Rowe's empty desk and chair did little to soothe his feelings. Why the hell did the Old Man have to take her along? The Attorney-General was still zealously protecting the

fair Amabel with all the show of a mother hen cluck-
ing over her young. Damn his hide! Angel scowled
darkly. He ignored the pair of US Marines on guard
outside the Attorney-General's office, and they,
recognizing him and taking note of his mood,
pretended not to notice as he shoved open the doors
and went in without knocking. Angel closed the
doors – none too quietly – and turned, the blunt
question rising on his lips:

'Just what the hell is going on?'

There was a slight pause. A silence.

'Thank you for coming so promptly, Mr Angel,'
said the President of the United States. 'Please sit
down.'

Angel snatched off his hat and subsided mutely
into the leather armchair facing the big oak desk. In
other times Angel and the Attorney-General had
locked horns in many a confrontation across that
very desk. Watching the President now, Angel
wondered if he was about to be drawn into yet
another.

'As you may know, Angel,' Rutherford B. Hayes
began, 'the Attorney-General is heading a high-level
discussion on law and judicial reform. The Supreme
Court judges and four United States senators are
with him. To ensure complete freedom from inter-
ruption the meetings . . . were being held on board a
special train.'

The President's deliberate hesitation got him
Angel's full, undivided attention.

'You did say *were* being held, Mr President?'

The President nodded. 'Three days ago a group of men boarded the train while it was taking on water at an isolated stop in Arizona. The four-man squad of soldiers who were travelling as escort were all killed and the train, plus its passengers, is now in the hands of these killers. We now know who they are.' The President picked up a sheet of paper from the desk and studied it, frowning. 'There are six of them. All are convicted men who broke out of Yuma Territorial Prison a week ago. Every one of them has killed. Every one of them is liable to kill again at any time. When they boarded the train they had no idea who was on it. Now they do and they have made it clear that if we don't give them what they want. . . .' The Presidential voice trailed off. 'Do I need to say more, Mr Angel?'

Angel sat upright, his mind racing.

'Just what are their demands?'

'Complete freedom from any further prosecution. A clean start for them all in a place of their choosing. Large cash ransom payments. The release of a number of their friends serving long sentences in various parts of the country. Horses. Clothing. The list is unreasonably long, but then these people realize the importance of the hostages they are holding.'

'Do we know where the train is now?' Angel asked.

'Not definitely. One of the conditions laid down was that any sign of pursuit or observation would

7

result in one of the hostages being killed. By the time we received the first of the telegraph messages from these people too much time had elapsed. It gave them the opportunity of moving the train off the main track and on to some isolated spurline. This is what the railroad people have come up with and I must agree that it sounds probable.'

'It's a hell of a big country out there,' Angel murmered. 'Are you going to agree to their terms, Mr President?'

The President smiled. 'The people on that train are important, Mr Angel. I do not think you would disagree. I would not like to think I might be responsible for their deaths. On the other hand I do not like being threatened by a gang of violent murderers who expect the United States Government to go down on its knees before their demands. It is a little ironical to think that the people on that train were there to discuss law and order. Now they have become pawns in a very serious trial of strength over that very matter. Tell me, Mr Angel, what would the Attorney-General have done in a situation like this?'

Now Angel knew why he'd been sent for. Now he had the answers, and he knew damn well that he'd soon be on his way.

'The Attorney-General's reaction would be pretty much the same as yours, Mr President. He doesn't like being threatened either. If he'd been sitting in that chair right now I know what he'd be saying. First he would start by gaining some time. He'd stall and he'd bluff. He'd get those men to thinking he was ready to negotiate. And while that was going on he'd have somebody on their way to deal with the situation.'

'The Attorney-General was right. He told me you thought along the same lines as himself. He said to me that if anything came up that couldn't be handled by the book to call in Frank Angel. He speaks very highly of you, Mr Angel. I hope his faith in you is justified because you may hold his life in your hands!'

'Do I understand that you're giving me control of this assignment, Mr President?'

The President nodded. 'There is a train waiting to take you wherever you want to go. Whatever you require just ask for. Additional personnel if you need them. We will do everything in our power to delay matters, Angel, and the moment you send word you can have what you need. I'm sure you realize as well as I do, Mr Angel, that the word of these men cannot be trusted. Even if we agreed to their every demand what guarantee would we have that they would honour their word?'

'None, Mr President, none at all,' Angel said, standing up. 'As far as I'm concerned they already have guns pointed at the heads of those hostages. The only thing that concerns me is whether I can get to them before they pull any triggers.'

'Then do it, Mr Angel!'

'My way,' Angel said. 'No interference and no questions!'

'Just get them out, Angel,' said the President. 'Get them out – alive!'

2

The President was as good as his word and Angel got what he wanted. On the stroke of noon, with rain slanting down from an overcast sky, Angel's special train pulled out of a siding at Washington's rail depot and eased onto the main line. Ahead lay close on 1800 miles of track: track that had been cleared all the way through to Arizona. A lot of people had been inconvenienced, timetables thrown out of the window, passenger and freight trains delayed, switched to other lines, and nobody knew why. A few high-ups knew where the orders had originated, yet even they had no notion of the reason behind all the fuss. There was a lot of grumbling, a lot of cursing, none of which did anything to change the situation. The big ten-wheeler, with only a single caboose coupled on behind, left the urban sprawl of the city in its wake as it picked up speed, thick smoke belching from the huge stack. It curved out across the green countryside, streaking towards the distant, humped peaks of the Appalachian range.

In the rear of the caboose Frank Angel, peering through a wet, soot-specked window, thought about what he was doing and where he was going: from the almost-civilized atmosphere of the capital, clear across country to the arid, sun-bleached wastes of Arizona, where he would no doubt have to take lives to save others. There were times when Frank Angel was convinced that the world was little more than a madhouse. A vast, teeming jungle with one rule: if you want to survive, to live in the way you want, then beat the rest down before they do it to you. Maybe his view of the world was coloured by his personal experiences. Maybe he was just a little weary of the never-ending parade of killers and gunmen he was constantly having to face. Maybe he was just concerned that two of the most important people in his life were in danger.

Which in truth was the one and only cause of his vexation.

Angel was fonder of both Amabel Rowe and the Attorney-General than he liked to own up to even to himself. They were his anchor, his point of return, his contact with sanity in an otherwise violent and restless world. It didn't matter what kind of hell he might crawl through during an assignment, what brutality he often sank to in order to stay alive. All he had to do was to walk in through the open doors of the Justice Department building and up the echoing, solid stairs, first to see the bright-eyed, beautiful young woman seated at her desk, then to step into the Old Man's great, book-lined office, with its vast desk and welcoming leather armchairs. There would be the Attorney-General himself, waiting, watching, listening, maybe ready to let fly with a thunderous reprimand, then maybe a gentle word of praise. For that Frank Angel would have walked clear to hell and back in his bare feet. Because once he reached the orderly calm of that rambling old building he knew that nothing could stop him. He was home. Like an adventurous boy who could lock the door against his fantasies, leaving them out in the dark and the cold, he was home.

But right now a man named Hugo Lyedekker was threatening that part of Angel's life. A violent and unpredictable man, leading a bunch of similar characters who were using the lives of good people as pawns in a deadly game. Hugo Lyedekker, with his base demands of money and personal desires, was willing to destroy if he did not get his way. Angel had read the Department's file on Lyedekker, plus the files of all the men with him, and he was in no doubt that if Lyedekker failed to force Washington to pay his ransom, then Amabel Rowe, the Attorney-General, and the other members of the party would all die. Lyedekker would kill them for pure spite. It was the way the man's mind worked. If he made a threat he would carry it through. He had done it before – and Angel saw no reason for Lyedekker suddenly to change his ways.

Angel turned away from the window, paced rest-

13

lessly back and forth across the swaying caboose. His two companions, relief engineer and fireman, who would take over from the present crew after a predetermined number of hours, viewed Angel's caged stalking with silent confusion. They had no knowledge of Angel's status, apart from the fact that he was an extremely important passenger who had to be transported to Arizona in the shortest possible time. They hadn't been told why. They were railmen. All they were concerned with was the physical challenge of hurling the train in their charge across the vast spread of miles to its arrival point. That was enough in itself. Steel and iron, steam and fire was their world. Coaxing an extra mile per hour out of a locomotive gave them satisfaction. The business of this cold-eyed, silent stranger, prowling around in the confines of the caboose, aroused minimal interest. Even that faded after a while, and the two railmen returned to their game of cards.

Slumped down on the bunk at the far end of the caboose Angel stared moodily at the oil-lamp swinging on its hook above his head. It would take somewhere in the region of forty hours, the railroad people had said. If the train could average sixty miles an hour, allowing for the minimum of stops for taking on water and refuelling, then forty hours should do it. Of course, they had added, hastily, there was nothing they could do about adverse weather conditions, or faults in the track, or locomotive failure. Then there were things like flash floods, landslides, falling trees across the track. Angel had walked out on them. What a way to run a railroad, he'd thought. Forty hours! Enough time for a man to die a thousand times over. More than enough time for . . . He sat up, swearing softly to himself, realizing he was beginning to think just like those doom merchants back in the railroad office.

He'd get there! Somehow he'd get there!

He took a walk to the front of the caboose, stepped through the door that led to the section of the car used for freight. A big, powerful chestnut mare turned its head to stare at him. Angel crossed to the horse and spoke to it. The animal responded to his words. Angel had picked the horse himself, going for an animal with plenty of staying power. There was no way of telling how far he might be forced to ride once he reached Arizona. It was a big country with a lot of empty spaces, and Angel wanted a horse he could trust. The only way to ensure that had been for him to pick it himself.

Satisfied that the horse had settled Angel returned to the main section of the caboose. He stood and watched the two railmen and their card-game for a while. Again, though, he felt the restless agitation steal over him. He crossed to the bunk again and lay down. He closed his eyes, relaxing, letting his mind and body drift. Clearing his mind of conscious thought turned out to be a difficult task. An image persisted. The image of a smiling young woman with blue eyes and honey-coloured hair. Damn you,

Amabel, he yelled mentally, don't make it harder than it is! The image drifted away – but was replaced by the face of the Attorney-General himself. He seemed to be scowling at Angel, as though he wasn't satisfied with the way things had turned out. Which would naturally have been the Old Man's reaction at being taken hostage, Angel thought, smiling to himself.

He breathed deeply, steadily, allowing his body to cast off its physical form. He slid away from reality, a formless entity, shut off from everything around him. He rested. It was a techique he had learned from the little Korean martial-arts instructor, Kee Lai, one of the mysterious Oriental practices that Angel had never fully mastered, but had come close to under-standing in principle if not in total application. As Kee Lai had once explained to him, the ways of the East were not to be grasped overnight. They took years, often a full, dedicated lifetime to perfect. What Angel learned stood him in good stead, giving him an unknown edge over his opponents. His way of life allowed him only brief periods of rest, snatched moments between assignments, but whenever the opportunity arose Angel sought out Kee Lai, probing the Korean's mind, studying, practising, developing his own skills. More than once he had fallen back on those skills, owing his life to some mystic technique, and Angel was the first to admit that even once was worth all the gruelling, bone-jarring, brutal punish-ment Kee Lai's training had entailed.

Later, still stretched out on the bunk, Angel went over the few facts he had. The train had disappeared somewhere between Tucson and Phoenix. Lyedekker couldn't have asked for a better place to take over a train. The vast, empty reaches of that part of Arizona were ideal. It was a sprawling, limitless expanse of wilderness, arid desertland, sunbaked, rocky mountains, all honeycombed by canyons and deep ravines, giving a million places to hide. It was desolate country. Very few people lived there – save the Apaches, who used the place to vanish into when they were on the run. According to the file Angel had read, Hugo Lyedekker knew the country pretty well, and digging a man out of his own backyard was always harder than taking him from somewhere where he was a stranger. Angel figured that Lyedekker would have abandoned the train by now. It would have served his purpose. After that it would have become superfluous to his needs. So he would have stripped it of everything useful and gone on into his wild country, seeking some place to rest and wait.

Lyedekker had to wait for an answer from Washington, which would come over the telegraph. Here, due to the quick-thinking of some distant telegraph operator, the Department had got its one thin line on the whereabouts of at least one of Lyedekker's men. When the message had first come through to Washington, the operator, obviously being forced into making it, had preceded his message with a priority code, alerting Washington that he was making a transmission against his will. He had also made sure that Washington was aware of his identity and his whereabouts. So, for as long as they could string along Lyedekker's man, Washington would keep sending messages, asking for more details, doing every damn thing they could, hoping to keep Lyedekker's messenger right where he was until Angel could arrive. Because that messenger was Angel's only lead to Lyedekker's hideout. If Angel could get to the man he would find out the information he required – one way or another.

At one of the infrequent stops, while the crews changed over and fuel was being taken on, Angel stepped inside the station's tiny telegraph office and showed the operator his badge. Within minutes a message was on its way to the Department of Justice. There was the inevitable delay before Angel received a reply. It was curt, to the point: WE WILL KEEP DELAY-ING AS LONG AS POSSIBLE STOP IMPERATIVE YOU MAKE CONTACT QUICKLY STOP DEPARTMENT OF JUSTICE WASH-INGTON. Angel snatched the message sheet from the operator's hand, dashed out of the office and back on board the train. As it drew out of the tiny station Angel read the terse communication again, then crumpled it up and tossed it out of the window. The wind tossed the flimsy paper aside. Angel shook his head. Imperative, that's what they'd said. Make contact quickly. What the hell did they expect him to do? Sprout wings and fly? A wry grin edged his taut mouth. He was Angel in name only. As far as he knew he hadn't any other attributes associated with his heavenly namesakes. Right there and then Angel found himself wishing he had. He could have used some help!

He spent most of the journey resting, or poring over minutely detailed maps that he had obtained from the Department's topographical section. The trouble with maps was their inability to render the kind of information Angel needed. They could show general land formations, the elevation of mountain ranges, the course of a river. But they could not show every canyon, ravine, valley, rim or mesa, or a dozen other features which might easily exist in a given area of land. Angel rolled up his maps and put them away. The only way he was going to learn what he needed to know was by extracting it from Lyedekker's man.

The journey took forty-four hours and the distance eventually worked out at nearer 2000 miles than the originally estimated 1800. Angel didn't worry. He was just thankful to arrive. The moment the train stopped he got the big caboose door open, dropped the ramp, and led his horse out into the early morning heat. He had already saddled the chestnut and his gear was fastened behind the saddle. Angel swung into the saddle as the caboose was closed up. He lifted a hand in a quick salute to the engine crew. He turned the horse away as the train began to back up, leaving him alone, seemingly in the middle of nowhere.

He had an hour's ride before he would reach

Fuller's Crossing, the place from where Lyedekker's demands had originated. Angel had learned that it was no more than a small settlement, consisting mainly of a trading post which also combined telegraph office, collection and delivery of goods for the railroad and at odd times even dealt with passengers. Fuller's Crossing, situated on the bank of a creek, sat squarely at a crossroads, where railroad and trails met.

Angel followed the steel rails, letting the restless chestnut find its own pace. He sat easy in his saddle, thankful to be out of the confines of the caboose. He felt the direct heat of the sun on his body, his eyes smarting from the reflected glare, and compared the harsh, unrelenting climate with that of Washington. No denying, Washington could get hot; but then it was the close, cloying smother only found in an overcrowded city: a musty, often unpleasant taint that was somehow hard to get rid of. Here it was hot, damned hot, and the land itself seemed set on doing everything it could to wear a man down. If it didn't bake him it would cover him with dust and if that failed there was always a lack of water. It was one hell of a place, Angel thought, but there was something about it that brought a man back, one way or another. He still had enough romance left in him to be able to appreciate a desert sunset. To breathe in the soft evening air touched with the smell of sage, to admire the stark beauty of soaring, silent canyons, the weird and wonderful formations of rocks, shaped by wind and weather over a thousand years. A man would have to be devoid of feeling not to see what lay just beneath the land's outer veneer of hostile savagery. But then, Angel thought, that veneer also hid more than a few dangers.

Fuller's Crossing had little appeal, even for a dedicated romantic. Squatting in the shade of a tall saguaro, Frank Angel studied the place through a pair of battered old field glasses. If he hadn't known better it would have been easy to imagine Fuller's Crossing to be deserted. There was nothing outside to indicate the presence of people. Nothing moved. No sound rose to his ears. The main building and the scattering of smaller outhouses stood mutely devoid of human presence. But there was a thin trail of smoke from the tall chimney at one end of the main building. And Angel caught a shadow of movement behind one of the windows.

He spent a long time watching, searching, but found nothing else to arouse his interest. The only way to find out what he wanted to know was by going down there. Angel eased back from his vantage point and crossed to his waiting horse. He put away the glasses and mounted up. He turned his horse on to the rutted trail that led to Fuller's Crossing, forded the shallow creek bypassing the place, and rode on in.

3

'Anybody home?'

Angel cuffed his stained hat to the back of his head, gazing casually round the empty yard, as if expecting an answer.

'Hey, there's a hungry man out here!'

The silence was thick enough to punch holes in. Angel leaned forward, patting the chestnut's glossy neck, sliding a quick glance in the direction of the main building. Nothing. He sighed with impatience. Come on, he begged, I know you bastards are in there!

The door creaked gently on dry hinges. Angel straightened up as it swung open. A lean, brown-faced man with bright blue eyes stepped outside. He gazed up at Angel as if he was some kind of apparition. As the man neared his horse Angel noticed a dark bruise on the left cheek.

'Can't do anything for you, mister,' the man said. He looked extremely nervous. 'Best you ride on. We got sickness here an' it's catchin'.' The man poked out a long-fingered hand, like some superstitious native warding off evil. 'For God's sake ... leave!' This time his tone was urgent.

'You the feller who sends telegraph messages?' Angel enquired.

The man frowned. Then he nodded.

'If you got something just write it down an' I'll do what I can when I get a chance.'

Angel's voice lowered. 'Next time you call the Justice Department tell them I got here. Now how many are there?'

The blue eyes flickered briefly.

'Two,' the man said, 'and they're both just inside, behind the door.'

Angel smiled. 'Well, I'm right grateful 'bout your warnin', friend,' he drawled. 'If you'll give me a minute I'll put down my message on a piece of paper an' be on my way. Sure do hope you get over your sickness.'

Angel turned his horse in towards the hitch rail. He swung lightly from the saddle and was momentarily hidden from view by the bulk of his horse. When he reappeared he was moving fast, coming from behind the chestnut at a dead run. His long legs took him the few yards to the open door in seconds. His right shoulder struck the door, driving it back against the inner wall, and as Angel hit the floor he heard a man's angry yell. Twisting his body as he rolled, Angel snatched at the Colt on his hip, thumb drawing back the hammer.

Coming up on one knee Angel saw the two men by the door. One was down on the floor, clutching his hands to his bloody face. The other had a gun in his hand, already pointed in Angel's direction. It spouted a red gout of flame, the sound of the shot loud in the confines of the room. Something shattered just behind Angel's left shoulder as he wrenched his body off to one side. He fired as he fell, saw his shot blast shreds of cloth from the man's shirt over his left arm. The man grunted, snatched his arm back, at the same time dragging his gun round. Angel triggered second and third shots, this time placing them with deliberate intent. The man shuddered under the impact, slamming back against the wall, blood spreading down his front from the holes in his chest. His legs suddenly gave and he pitched forward on to his face. His gun bounced from his hand, clattering noisily on the floorboards.

Angel stood up. He crossed over to the other man and snatched the unused gun from his holster. He reached down and took hold of the man's shirt, hauling him roughly to his feet, driving him back against the wall.

'Put the hands down, friend,' Angel said.

'You broke my goddam nose,' the man mumbled through bloody fingers.

Angel rapped him sharply across the knuckles with the barrel of his Colt.

'I said put the hands down!'

The man dropped his hands from his face. Blood

streamed from his nose, which lay flattened, crushed out of shape. In his battered, pockmarked face it made little difference to his appearance. Despite the man's injury Angel had no difficulty in recognizing him.

Floyd Dagget. One of Hugo Lyedekker's old partners in crime. Dagget was no thinking man. Simply a bully-boy who was good at one thing only. Hurting people. In a variety of ways.

Angel backed off, leaving Dagget to stand uncertainly against the wall.

'You all right?'

It was the man who had come outside to meet Angel. He paused as he stepped inside, his eyes drawn to the dead man sprawled bloodily on the floor.

'Sorry about the mess,' Angel said.

'Sorry? Hell, mister, what have you got to apologize for?' The man held out a hand, then realized Angel's difficulty in responding while he was holding a gun. 'I'm John Myer. I run this place.'

'Frank Angel.'

'Thank God you turned up, Mr Angel,' Myer said. 'The last few days have been ... frankly, goddam awful!'

'John Myer, I'll ask you to refrain from using such language in this house!'

Out of the corner of his eye Angel saw a woman appear from the next room. She moved round to stand next to Myer, nodding in Angel's direction.

She was in her late thirties, dark-haired, with the worn look of a woman who has spent the best of her life in a land apt to be harsher on women than man. Yet she still managed to retain a feminine attractiveness that Angel couldn't help noticing.

'This is my wife Olivia,' John Myer said, slipping an arm round the woman's slender waist.

'Glad to see you're unharmed, ma'am.'

Olivia Elyer threw a bitter glance in Dagget's direction.

'No thanks to him and his late friend!'

'What's your next move, Mr Angel?' Myer asked.

Angel gestured in Dagget's direction.

'I need somewhere private to have a talk to our ugly friend . . . and I mean private!' He glanced at Olivia Myer. 'Ma'am, I need to know things from him and he'll tell me, one way or the other.'

Olivia Myer's face paled slightly, but she nodded.

'I understand what you mean, Mr Angel. I may not wholly approve but you do what you have to. That man won't get my sympathy.'

'There's a stable out back,' Myer suggested.

Angel nodded. He crossed to where Dagget stood.

'Let's go, Dagget.'

'Where?' Dagget demanded.

'Outside.'

Dagget's cold eyes narrowed in suspicion.

'What's out there I need to see?'

There was no warning of Angel's next move. He simply reached up and caught hold of Dagget's shirt,

26

spun the man round and propelled him through the door. Dagget missed the step and pitched headlong on to the ground, cursing wildly. Angel followed him, booting Dagget brutally in the side, wrenching a howl of pain from the man.

'On your feet, Dagget!' Angel yelled. 'Move!'

Dagget staggered to his feet. He stared at Angel, unconcealed violence gleaming in his eyes. For a moment it looked as if he might ignore the gun being pointed at him. But he held back, pawing at the sticky mess of blood and dirt streaking his face.

'Over to the stable, mister,' Angel demanded.

Dagget weaved his uncertain way across the dusty yard. He dragged open the stable door on Angel's instruction and they moved inside. Angel dragged the sagging door shut, dropping the interior bar in place. Dagget watched him, his face creased by a deep frown.

'What the hell's goin' on?' he asked.

'It's question and answer time, Dagget,' Angel told him. 'I ask them and you tell me what I want to know.'

Dagget spat on the dirt floor.

'An' what if I don't?' he sneered.

A soft sigh came from Angel. Almost reluctantly he brought up his left fist in a wide loop and sledged a hard blow to the side of Dagget's jaw. Dagget's head snapped round under the impact, his eyes bulging with surprise. He fell to one side and came up hard against the side of an empty stall. He threw up one

27

hand to grab hold of the side of the stall and hung there, blood dripping from his mouth.

Angel glanced at his skinned knuckles. He hoped that Dagget didn't make too many problems.

'You son of a bitch!' Dagget said softly, but with great feeling. He shoved himself away from the stall, swaying as he stared at Angel. 'If you didn't have that gun in your hand I'd beat your ass off!'

'Probably you would, Dagget, but I ain't about to give you the chance. Now, you feel like telling me what I want to hear? Or do we get to kick you round some more?'

'Go to hell!' Dagget snarled. 'You just go to . . . !'

This time Angel hit him in the stomach. Hard and fast, before Dagget could do a thing to protect himself. Dagget let out a choked grunt, folding forward. Angel let him get so far down then drove the toe of his boot in Dagget's side. This time it was a scream. Dagget hit the floor in a writhing tangle of arms and legs. He lay moaning softly, hugging his body with spread hands.

Angel stepped back out of sight and left Dagget to it. Five minutes drifted by. Dagget had fallen silent now. He wasn't moving. He was waiting, looking for a chance, an opportunity to take Angel. Angel didn't give him an opening. He just stood by until Dagget got tired of lying on the floor. Dagget eventually raised his head, peered round, then paused when he couldn't locate Angel. He got up slowly, cautiously . . . not certain whether he was alone or not. His

28

curiosity was swiftly and mercilessly satisfied. A hard hand took hold of his hair, yanked back his head and dragged him back until he was rammed up against the end of the stall. Then, even while Dagget's dazed senses were trying to sort themselves out, he saw something which brought a cold shiver to his spine.

It was the cold, clean gleam of a slim-bladed knife held in Angel's right hand, the honed steel tip lifted so that Dagget could see it clearly. Behind the blade Angel's expressionless eyes fixed themselves on Dagget.

'I'll let you make the choice, Dagget,' he said gently.

'What you goin' to do wi . . . ?' Dagget bit his words off. He didn't need to ask. The knife had moved, vanishing from his field of vision. And then he felt the sharp prick of the blade as the tip nudged the taut flesh of his throat.

'You feel like talking, Dagget, you better do it now, 'cause it ain't going to be that easy after I've cut your throat!'

'You ain't got the guts!' Dagget blurted out, anger and frustration causing his outburst. Then a yell of pure fright exploded from his lips as he felt a stinging pain run across his throat. He felt warm blood ooze down his flesh, soaking his shirt.

'Still figure I can't do it?' Angel asked.

'Jesus Christ, mister, you must be crazy! What the hell you doin' to me?' Dagget swore wildly, but he made no attempt to move because he could feel the

29

knife at his throat again.

'Then quit wastin' my time,' Angel snapped.

Dagget fell silent for a minute. He finally admitted to himself that if he wanted to get out of this alive then he was going to have to start thinking of saving his own skin. Lyedekker and the others would have to do the same when the time came.

'So ask your questions,' he said bitterly.

'Wasn't so bad after all was it?' Angel asked. He let go of Dagget and stepped back, the knife moving to his left hand, the Colt appearing again in his right. 'Where's Lyedekker holed up?'

'In the Maricopas. There's a dead town up there. Used to be silver-mines or somethin'. Years back. When the mines played out everybody left. Lyedekker's used it before.'

'This place got a name?'

'They called it Hope.'

'What about the hostages?' Angel asked. 'Anyone been hurt?'

Dagget shook his head. 'Not before I left. Hell, one or two of 'em got shoved around when they got mule-headed.'

'The girl?'

'Ain't nobody touched her far as I know.' Dagget peered closely at Angel. 'Hell, she somethin' special or what?'

Angel hit him in the mouth. The sudden shock of the blow put Dagget on his back in the dirt. He lay there, cursing Angel bitterly.

30

'Shit, you son of a bitch, you could of put the gun down first!'

It was only then that Angel realized he had the Colt in his hand.

'Get up, Dagget.'

Angel opened the stable door and prodded the bleeding, protesting man back across the yard. John Myer came out to meet him. He eyed Dagget's battered condition with something close to satisfaction.

'Myer, you got anywhere we can put this?' Angel asked, indicating the surly Dagget. 'Somewhere he won't get out?'

Myer nodded. 'There's a cellar under the house. Only one way in. Through a trap-door in the living-room floor.'

'That'll do.'

Myer led the way through the house. He dragged aside a heavy table and exposed the trap-door. He slid back the bolt and lifted the door.

'I ain't goin' down there,' Dagget grumbled.

'Dagget,' Angel said, and when the man looked at him Angel clouted him with the barrel of his gun. Dagget folded up and slid to the floor. With Myer's help Angel got Dagget down into the cellar. When they climbed out Angel pulled up the ladder, closed the trap-door and bolted it. 'And don't let him out, no matter what. If you have to feed him pass it down. Don't give him a chance to get out.'

Myer smiled. 'If he tries I'll shoot him.'

'Now you're getting the idea. Look, I'd like to send a report back to Washington. Can you clear the line?'

'Sure,' Myer said. He led the way through to the small office containing the telegraph and sat down, shoving a blank pad across to Angel. By the time they left the office Angel had informed Washington of his progress, and the Department was arranging for the local US marshal to come out to Fuller's Crossing to take charge of Dagget.

'So what will you do now?' Myer asked over a cup of coffee.

They were sitting in the neatly organized kitchen, with Olivia Myer preparing a hot meal.

'Dagget told me where the hostages are being held. So I reckon I'll be making my way there.'

'On your own?' Myer asked.

Angel stirred more sugar into his coffee.

'It's the way I work, Mr Myer.'

'The name's John, and you're talking cragy. Why don't you wait for the US marshal? I'm sure he could—'

Olivia Myer banged a plate down on the table before her husband.

'I'm sure that Mr Angel knows his business best, John. I dare say he's faced problems like this before.'

'Too many times,' Angel confirmed. 'Thanks for your concern, John, but you don't need to worry. The Department's investigators are trained to work solo. Each man tackles his assignment his own way, but within the jurisdiction of the Department.'

'Well I hope you find those hostages safe and well,' Olivia said. She served out thick slices of fried ham, eggs, brown potatoes. 'It must be terrible for them, and especially for that young woman.'

'Yes, ma'am,' Angel said.

Olivia caught the expression in his eyes, and realized that there was more to it than just official concern.

'You must think a lot of her,' she said gently.

'Yes, I do, ma'am,' Angel said. 'Can't hide a thing from a woman, can we?'

Olivia smiled. 'That's the trouble with you men. You figure you've got the world by the horns. But none of you is as tough as you think. Or as smart!'

Angel glanced across at John Myer.

'I'm beginning to wonder who runs this place.'

Myer grinned. 'I do when there are customers about. But when we're alone I'm just a general skivvy to the boss here!'

Olivia laughed, a bright, warm sound, and it reminded Angel of Amabel Rowe. Her image thrust its way into his thoughts, so vivid he could almost reach out and touch it. But he could do little more than sit and wonder about her. Try to imagine what she was doing at that very moment.

4

'No! I won't!'

'My dear, I understand how you feel. But stubborn pride isn't going to fill your stomach.'

'Then I'll go hungry!'

'Talk like that doesn't do any good. Be practical, my dear. I agree that the food is disgusting. Badly cooked and practically indigestible. But while we are in our present circumstances I am not expecting anything above the level of bad camp-fire cooking.'

'Then you eat the damned stuff because I won't!'

'Amabel!'

The stern voice filled the small, cramped room, seeming to even rattle the filthy panes of glass in the single window.

Amabel Rowe realized she had gone too far. She shrank back from the solemn gaze of the Attorney-General, wishing she was a hundred miles from this terrible place. Even fifty would do! How she needed to get out of this place. The desire was becoming almost too strong to live with, but Amabel was level-

34

headed enough to realize that matters weren't resolved simply because you wished them to be!

'Sit down, my dear,' the Attorney-General said. 'Let's talk. It might help.'

'Of course,' Amabel remarked lightly. 'We could also sing songs of a rousing and uplifting nature! Perhaps that might help!'

The Attorney-General smiled. 'When you say things like that, Amabel, I can see Frank Angel leering at me over your shoulder. It's the kind of disrespectful remark that young man would come out with.'

'Disrespectful or not, I wish he was here right now.'

'Keep that thought in your mind, my dear, because it might not be as wild as you think.'

Amabel's eyes sparkled. The first time in days she's shown any interest, thought the Attorney-General, and found he was extremely envious of one Frank Angel.

'Do you know something I don't?' Amabel asked.

'My dear young woman, there are many things I know of which you are unaware. In answer to your question – it is not outside the bounds of possibilty that Mr Angel might very well be searching for us. And though I often have doubts about the lawfulness of his methods, there is a chance he may locate us.'

'But how?'

'I can see you need a refresher course on Department policy. There are certain procedures laid down covering all eventualities. The Department will have put the wheels in motion.'

'We are a long way from Washington,' Amabel pointed out.

'Have you no faith in the Department?'

'Faith isn't going to deal with those outlaws!' Amabel said.

'No. Faith is not going to bring us out of here. I expect help to be of a more practical nature. If nothing else, Angel has a penchant for practicality. It may be that for the first time since he joined the Department Angel will be able to demonstrate his abilities to me at first hand.' The Attorney-General reflected on his words, adding: 'It is a daunting prospect, my dear.'

'I can't see that man Lyedekker giving up without a fight, sir.'

'Hugo Lyedekker values his freedom. Any threat to that freedom will be met with extreme hostility. The same applies to the rest of his unsavoury companions.'

Amabel reluctantly picked up her spoon, using it to prod the congealing mess of beans and greasy meat on her plate. She took a quick mouthful and found that it was as bad as she had imagined. Frank Angel, she implored silently, if you are coming to get us out of here, for heaven's sake be quick about it. I can't stand many more meals like this.

'It appears we have a visitor,' the Attorney-General said from his position at the window.

Amabel glanced up quickly, hoping against hope. She caught the Attorney-General's warning glance and returned to her meal as the door was unlocked, then thrown open.

'Now ain't this cosy!'

Hugo Lyedekker leaned against the doorpost, a wide smirk on his broad, square face. He was a heavy-set man, not tall, so that his overall appearance seemed out of proportion. His hands were unusually large, with powerful, thick fingers. A dense mass of dark hair hung almost to his broad shoulders. The Attorney-General had summed him up as a volatile man, even unstable. Lyedekker was prone to moods of wild rage if things appeared to be going against him, and beneath the surface lurked a violent side to his character.

'Ejoying your meal, honey?' Lyedekker asked, moving into the room.

Amabel raised her head, blue eyes flashing angrily.

'It may satisfy your taste, Mr Lyedekker,' she said,'but I am not used to being served with pigswill!'

Lyedekker's face darkened, then true to his character his mood changed.

'Well now, honey, you'll just have to get used to living at our level for the time being.' He chuckled softly. 'Why, give you a few more days and you'll be down on your knees in the dirt with the rest of us.'

'I doubt that very much, Mr Lyedekker. If I spent the rest of my life trying I couldn't get as low as you!'

'Bitch!' Lyedekker snapped. His left hand swung

up and slapped Amabel across the face.

'Lyedekker!' The Attorney-General's voice crack-led with authority. He took three long strides and caught hold of the outlaw's sleeve.

'Get your hands off me!' Lyedekker yelled. He put one big hand against the Attorney-General's chest and pushed him aside. He turned back to face Amabel, and that was when she hit him in the face with the plate of food. Lyedekker gave a howl of anger, clawing at the sticky mess covering his eyes.

Amabel leaned forward and snatched the heavy revolver from Lyedekker's holster. She put all her strength behind a wild swing that laid the barrel against Lyedekker's exposed skull, just above his ear. Lyedekker grunted, stumbling against the table, and Amabel hit him again. Lyedekker went down to the floor, moaning softly.

'Give me that thing!'

Amabel glanced at the Attorney-General and his outstretched hand. She gave him the gun and watched him check it expertly.

'Like it or not,' he said, 'you have started some-thing we'll have to see through. Now come on. Stay close to me and do exactly what I tell you!'

They paused in the open door of the small hut. On the rocky slope before them lay the long-deserted town of Hope. An unlovely hotch-potch of buildings that were for the most part in total disrepair. Doors were gone. Roofs had fallen in. Thick clumps of weeds grew up between the boardwalk planks. It was a sorry place, aptly summed up by the few letters some departing wit had carved in the weathered sign standing at the edge of town. At its birth the town had been given a name which summed up the feelings of the people who had come to this lonely place. It expressed their longing. HOPE. After the first flush of success the rot had set in and the rich veins of ore dwindled to nothing. The people drifted away, moving to fresh pastures, leaving the town to wither and die. And a few carved letters said it all. Just four, added to the name. Renaming it even as it died. Now the sign read: HOPELESS.

'Can we free the others?' Amabel asked.

'We can try,' the Attorney-General said. He led the way along the uneven path. His destination was another hut, some twelve yards off. Here the rest of the hostages were being held. Even if he managed to free them the Attorney-General wasn't sure what they would all do. Eight of them, alone in a wild and hostile land. They were all city-dwellers, not used to the harsh regime of this remote territory. Negotiating the muddy strip of Pennsylvania Avenue on a rainy day was the nearest any of them ever came to personal hardship. But, by God, if they managed to get clear of this place, the Attorney-General thought, the whole bunch of them would have to look to their laurels. Himself included! At least it would sort out the men from the boys. But they had to try. Even if help was on the way, it was ridiculous to just sit back and wait. The Attorney-General had no illusions. He had realised from the start that Hugo Lyedekker was capable of killing any and all of them if the mood struck him. And if anything went wrong with his arrangements he would do just that. The man had made it clear to them all. They were useful to him only for as long as he needed them. After that they became excess baggage, to be discarded at will. And with a man like Lyedekker that would mean a quick bullet in the back of the head.

'Damn!' the Attorney-General exclaimed. He stared at the heavy lock securing the door of the second hut.

'Would this help?' Amabel asked. She held up a pair of keys on a thin loop of rawhide. 'I took them from the lock on the door of our hut as we came out.'

'Amabel, how would I ever manage to run the Department without you?'

She glanced up from unlocking the door. 'With great difficulty,' she said.

The Attorney-General pushed open the door and stepped inside.

'Gentlemen, in words to suit the situation, let's get the hell out of here!'

The six men crowded together in the small hut moved towards the door. They stared at the Attorney-General as if he was some kind of liberating benefactor.

'How'd you do it, Charles?' asked Senator Orrin Whipple. He was a lean, taciturn individual, raised in Texas, but he had been in Washington for so long he'd almost forgotten his origins.

'When we have the time for discussions I'll tell you. At the moment all I want to do is get us all away from this place.'

'Ain't nobody goin' anywhere!'

They all looked towards the speaker.

Hugo Lyedekker. His face still bore the remnants of the food from Amabel's plate. There was a livid bruise discolouring the left side of his face from where he had hit the floor, and blood glistened wetly in the dark hair behind his right ear.

'You've all had your fun, boys, but playtime's over!' Lyedekker gestured abruptly and two of his men, holding rifles, moved into view. Stepping forward Lyedekker placed himself in front of the Attorney-General. 'I'll have my gun back now!'

The Attorney-General sighed. He handed the revolver to Lyedekker, who was grinning wolfishly, enjoying every second.

'You almost made it,' he said. 'But it was a stupid thing to do. How long do you figure you would have lasted out there? No food. No water. You all so ready to die? Hell, I can fix that for you right here and now. No takers? You disappoint me, boys.' He smiled indulgently. 'Back inside. All of you. Except the little lady. I got business with her.'

'Are you sure you can handle me all by yourself?' Amabel asked drily.

Lyedekker swung round on her, his face taut with anger.

41

'Smartmouth bitch!' he sneered. 'Fancy talk and fancy clothes: what you need, honey, is a man to settle you down!'

'Oh, are you going to find me one, Mr Lyedekker?'

The insult stung Lyedekker. He lashed out blindly, his big hand catching Amabel across the face. The force of the blow knocked her against the side of the hut. There wasn't a thing she could do against his brutal attack, and for a time there was no other sound apart from the solid crack of flesh against flesh.

'Mitch,' Lyedekker said at last, 'take her down below. Put her in one of the rooms where we can keep an eye on her, and if she starts up again you know what to do!'

5

He was somewhere in the parched wilderness of the rising foothills of the Maricopas. These were part of the vast tract of land which itself was a section of the Great Sonoran Desert, a gigantic sprawl of desert and semi-arid land engulfing an area of Arizona and spilling across the border into Mexico. The featureless rise of the Maricopas hung over Frank Angel as he prepared himself a quick meal, camped on the bank of a sluggish creek winding its way down out of the hills at his back. It was the first water he'd come across in two days, and Angel was ready for the opportunity to rest his horse and himself.

The dusty peaks of the mountains rose in uneven file to the north-west. Beyond them, further to the west, lay the Sand Tank and the Sauceda ranges. Many miles to the north would be the Gila River. It was hellish country to cross, Angel had decided after the first day. It was not the kind of terrain to be lost in. As far as he was concerned the Apaches could keep this damn place!

43

He was ready to dish out his food when he heard the riders coming.

Angel glanced over his shoulder and saw them. They were riding in his direction, and the moment he set eyes on them he sensed trouble.

There were three of them. They were, without exception, the filthiest, roughest, ugliest three men Angel had ever seen. They all wore greasy, blackened buckskins, fringed and ragged, with knee-high moccasins. Battered, sweaty, frayed hats were jammed on over matted hair that hung down shoulder-length.

Angel watched them ride in and draw rein. Three pairs of dark eyes surveyed him with open hostility. After a couple of minutes of acute silence had passed Angel figured he'd had enough nonsense so he commenced spooning food onto his plate.

'I was you, boy, I wouldn't bother,' one of the three said.

Angel, still spooning, glanced up.

'Now why would that be?'

The man who had spoken, the middle one of the trio, smiled, showing big, stained teeth. There was no humour in the smile.

'Dependin' on how you behave in the next couple of minutes, boy, you're either goin' to be ridin' out – or dead!'

'This private land?' Angel asked. 'Or have I missed something?'

The rider on Angel's left suddenly spat. He made

the simple function look potentially threatening.

'He's got a smart mouth, Luke! One thing I can't abide is a smart mouth!'

The one called Luke leaned forward in his saddle.

'You ain't made a good start there, boy! You get Charly riled up an' you're goin' to find the day turnin' a tad sour on you.'

'Let's get one thing straight, friend,' Angel said. 'I don't know you and I ain't all that bothered about finding out. I aim to finish my meal, break camp, and ride on. As far as I'm concerned you boys can do the same. So you can quit the fancy games. I'm not interested.'

'Just where are you headed, boy?' Luke asked, his tone abruptly cold, flat.

'My business,' Angel told him.

'Seems to me you're headin' up into the Maricopas,' Luke said. He scratched at his unshaven chin. 'Ain't nothin' up there 'cept hot rocks and snakes. So what you lookin' for, boy?'

'I'm looking to mind my own damn business!' Angel snapped. 'Try doing the same!'

'Goddam it, Luke, quit pussyfootin' around,' the one called Charly scowled. 'I reckon he's on the same trail we are.'

'That right, boy?' Luke asked. 'You out here to do a spot of hunting?'

'For two-legged game most likely!' Charly added.

Angel ignored the remark. He had these three marked now. They were bounty hunters and they

45

were searching for Lyedekker and his bunch. Which added up to trouble for Angel. The kind of trouble he could do without.

'Maybe you don't know who we are, boy,' Luke said. 'I'm Luke Quint. These here are my brothers – Charly and Perce. You know the names, boy? If you do then you ain't goin' to need no more tellin'.'

'If you don't,' Charly said smugly, 'then we'll oblige and make it right clear to you!'

Angel wasn't familiar with the Quints, but he understood the implications behind their words. They figured themselves to be some kind of celebrities. Men to be reckoned with. Which impressed Angel not at all.

'Hell, Luke,' Perce Quint said, 'either this son of a bitch is dumb, else he figures he's too smart for us.' He seemed angry at the possibility, edging his horse closer in towards Angel. 'That it, you son of a bitch? You figure you're smart enough to come to our territory and take what's ours?'

'Mister, you're doin' all the talking,' Angel said.

'Ahh, the hell with this!' Charly Quint yelled, slamming in his heels and sending his horse lunging forward.

Angel saw the looming bulk of the animal and tried to step aside. He almost made it but as it passed the horse's rear end nudged him. There was enough force to send Angel spinning to one side. He missed his footing and fell, hitting the dusty ground with a hefty whack. He rolled over, dazed, spitting dust, and feeling the anger starting to boil.

'Hahh! Go git him, Charly boy!'

Angel sat up, blinking his eyes to clear them. Somewhere he could hear the drum of a horse's hoofs, and the sound seemed to be getting closer. He twisted round, starting to climb to his feet. That was when he saw Charly Quint riding at him. For a moment Angel thought the man was going to trample him, but Charly took his horse off to one side. He was grinning wildly, yelling fit to bust, and only at the last moment did Angel see the rope in Charly's hands. A wide loop dropped over his shoulders, drew taut as Charly rode on by, the end of the rope snugged around his saddle horn. Rope twanged as it took Angel's weight, yanking him off his feet.

And then Angel was dragged helplessly behind Charly Quint's horse, bouncing and sliding across the hard, dusty ground. . . .

There wasn't a damn thing Angel could do. His arms were pinned at his sides by the rope. All he could do was put up with whatever Charly intended. Until Charly decided to stop.

The harsh surface of the ground burned his flesh, shredding his pants and shirt, scraping the exposed parts of his body. Choking on the dust kicked up by Charly's horse Angel suffered the ordeal in smouldering silence.

It stopped as quickly as it had started. As Charly's horse was halted Angel slithered to an uncomfortable stop himself, and lay, face down in the dust, curled up in a seemingly pain-racked position.

He heard Charly dismount. Could hear the man's insane giggling as Charly moved towards him.

'Hey, boy, you enjoy your trip? You want some more? Hell, I ain't even raised a sweat yet!'

Charly was still giggling as he reached Angel's prone figure. There was no response and Charly swore softly. He nudged Angel's body with his foot.

'Aw, come on there, boy,' Charly grumbled. 'Don't quit on me already! Shit, I just got started!'

Wrong, Angel said mentally.

And with that thought Angel uncoiled, driving the tip of his right boot up into Charly's stomach. There was a long, drawn out scream of agony as Charly was smashed backwards. Angel flexed his shoulders and spread the slack loop of rope, freeing himself from its grip. He rolled to his feet, stepping in to meet Charly's half-hearted resistance. White-faced and groaning Charly swung a meaty fist in Angel's direction. The blow was wide. Angel's wasn't. He drove brutal fists at Charly's face, felt flesh split under the impact. Charly stumbled away from him, blood streaming from his mouth and cheek.

There was a rush of noise behind him. Angel spun on his heel and saw Perce Quint in the act of hurling himself from the back of his running horse. Perce's heavy bulk smashed into Angel. The pair of them went down, Perce howling like a mad dog. He clawed and punched at Angel, using a lot of energy to little effect. Thrusting a stiffened palm upwards, Angel

48

snapped Perce's head back, the heel of his hand wedged under the man's lower jaw. Perce grunted, his hands scrabbling empty air. Angel shoved Perce to one side, rolling the man off him. Angel was on his feet first, turning to where Perce was on hands and knees in the dust. Perce was coughing, trying to draw air down his bruised throat. Angel slammed the sole of his boot down on the back of Perce's neck, smashing Perce's face against the ground. Perce flopped like a stranded fish, then lay still and quiet.

In the acute silence following Perce's forced retirement Angel caught a faint, unmistakable sound. Luke Quint was still in the game it seemed, and he was playing by different rules. Angel didn't hesitate. He let himself drop, twisting his body as he touched the ground. His right hand had already drawn the Colt and it was cocked and ready by the time he laid his eyes on Luke Quint.

The long-barrelled revolver in Luke's hand blasted a single shot. The bullet struck the ground well clear of Angel's body. A hasty shot. The kind that could get a man killed before he could loose another.

Angel fired a split second later. He saw Luke Quint go back a couple of steps. Luke dropped his gun and clapped a hand to his right shoulder, blood staining his fingers.

Angel climbed to his feet, keeping his gun in clear sight, the implication being that he was more than ready to use it again.

'You boys had enough or do you want me to get rough?'

'Son of a bitch,' Charly Quint mumbled through crushed, bloody lips. 'You was askin' for trouble!'

Angel smiled coldly. 'No. Not me, friend. But you boys were bound and determined to give me some. Seems everything got turned around.'

Charly had struggled to his feet. He glared at Angel as he stood swaying back and forth. 'God damn it, you went and shot Luke!'

'Hell, you noticed,' Angel said.

'I ought to . . .' Charly began. He fell silent as he became aware of the gun in Angel's hand. 'You shouldn't have shot Luke,' he finished lamely.

'Seemed like a good idea at the time,' Angel observed. 'Still looks that way.'

By the time Luke reached them, Perce had recovered enough to sit up. His face was a bruised and bloody mess.

'First thing, boys,' Angel said, 'is to get rid of all those guns and knives you're carrying. Toss 'em in the creek there. Be less of a temptation for you.'

There were muttered threats and strongly worded opinions concerning the legality of Angel's birth, but under the influence of Angel's unwavering gun the Quints went along with his request.

'I ain't about to forget this, mister,' Luke Quint said. 'There'll be a reckonin' due.'

'I wouldn't bother,' Angel suggested. 'Hell, there are only the three of you.'

'You ain't so tough!' Charly Quint yelled, his face dark with anger.

'I can live with it.' Angel used his free hand to free the badge he carried in his belt. He flashed it before Luke Quint's eyes. 'You know what that is?'

Luke Quint read the words emblazoned around the badge's perimeter. He glanced at Angel, cleared his throat and spat on the ground by Angel's boot.

'What is it, Luke?' Charly asked.

'The son of a bitch is a pissass lawman! A fancy boy from the Justice Department!'

'And that means stay away,' Angel warned. 'Forget about Lyedekker and his bunch. There isn't any bounty waitin' to be picked up.'

'The hell you say!' Charly exploded. 'Stuff you and your damn badge, you bastard! Luke, he's warning us off so's he can walk in and take the money!'

'That the way it is, boy?' Luke Quint asked. 'Can't say I take to that notion.'

'Well, boys, you can take it any damn way you want. Just keep your distance and don't make problems for me. You step on my toes I'll make you sorry you ever laid eyes on me.'

Luke grinned, despite the pain from his bloody shoulder.

'Mister, I been around this neck of the woods for a long time. Before there was any kind of law 'cept a man's own. I been gettin' along real fine, an' I ain't about to let some asshole with a shiny badge scare me off. You got the winnin' hand right now. But don't

51

figure you got Luke Quint beat.'

Angel backed off to where his horse stood. He gathered his gear and put it away, checked his saddle and mounted up. He pushed his horse up the long slope before him, not looking back until he'd covered a good quarter-mile. Below him he could see the Quints gathered round the small fire he'd left. He knew with absolute certainty that they would be down there drying out their weapons, tending to their wounds, cursing him to hell and back. And Angel knew, with just as much certainty, that he hadn't seen the last of the Quints.

6

'I still reckon something's gone wrong!'

Hugo Lyedekker banged his coffee-mug hard down on the table, spilling hot liquid over the back of his hand. He threw a murderous glance in the speaker's direction.

'For Christ's sake, Sam,' he stormed. 'It's getting like an old ladies' home around here! What's given everybody the shits? We're sittin' pretty and things'll get better when Washington starts payin'.'

'Sure, Hugo, it sounds fine the way you say it. But this ain't no fairy tale. How'd we know Washington's going to play along? They might be stringing us out to dry. Just delaying so they can send the law, maybe the army. What do we do the mornin' we wake up an' find the cavalry surrounding this place?' Sam Huffaker shook his head. 'We should have heard from Dagget or Crown by now. Hell, Hugo, maybe they ain't even there at Fuller's Crossing. Maybe they ran out on us. Maybe a posse caught up with 'em. . . .'

'Maybe . . . maybe . . .' Lyedekker mocked. 'Maybe if I fart in tune the Stars and Stripes'll come out my asshole! Drop it, Sam, you're gettin' on my goddam nerves.' Lyedekker stood up suddenly, almost over-turning the table. 'Look, if you don't like it why not ride out? No hard feelings. Just leave.'

Huffaker stared at him silently, his face devoid of any expression. Then he smiled, almost guiltily. 'You know I wouldn't quit, Hugo. We been together too long, you and me. We go way back.'

'So what's all the fuss about?' Lyedekker said. 'Trust me, Sam, I ain't ever let you down yet. Have I?'

Huffaker shook his head. 'I guess I'm a little jumpy. Hell, you know me, Hugo. I don't like it too quiet. This place gives me the creeps. I need a town with bright lights and noise.'

'Damnit, Sam, when this all comes through you'll be able to buy your own town.'

Huffaker got up. He put on his hat, picked up his rifle and made for the door.

'I'll go and relieve one of the boys. Give 'em a chance to get a bite to eat.'

'Sure, Sam,' Lyedekker said. 'And, Sam . . . don't worry.'

The door closed behind Huffaker's lean figure. Hugo Lyedekker picked up his coffee, turning away from the table.

And looked directly into the eyes of Amabel Rowe.

He had almost forgotten her presence. She was sitting in a big leather armchair, regarding him with a faintly amused expression on her badly bruised, swollen face.

'You find something to laugh at?' Lyedekker asked.

'Only you and that man, Huffaker.'

'Sam? Me?' Lyedekker studied her, puzzled. 'What's there to laugh at?'

'Just the way you're all fooling yourselves into believing everything is going to work out fine.'

'And you know different?'

'I don't think you're going to get away with it,' Amabel said. 'The only thing you'll get out of this is a rope around your neck. Or perhaps a bullet if you're lucky.'

Lyedekker grinned. 'My, quite the little expert. And how do you see yourself coming out of all this?'

'Alive and well, I hope.'

'Then I'd watch my mouth, honey,' Lyedekker warned. 'Next time you might not get off so light.'

Anger gleamed in Amabel's blue eyes.

'Mr Lyedekker, if I were a man—'

'Honey, if you were a man I'd be downright disappointed.' Lyedekker grinned. 'But if it'll help I'll lend you a gun and we'll step outside.'

'If I get mad enough I might accept your offer!' Amabel retorted. She stood up, trying to ignore the stiffness in her body, the nagging ache reminding her of the beating Lyedekker had administered. It had been sound and efficiently brutal. Hard enough to hurt and be remembered, but not severe enough to cause lasting damage. 'Do you mind if I go to my room?'

'Go ahead,' Lyedekker said. He watched her cross the room. 'You get lonely, honey, just yell!'

Half-way through the door of the small room, with its heavily boarded window and uncomfortable bed, Amabel glanced over her shoulder at Lyedekker.

'Nobody, Mr Lyedekker, could get that lonely!'

Lyedekker swore softly as the door closed. He spun round and stalked to the front window, staring out at the empty, rutted, weed-choked street. Damn, he thought, why don't the bastards answer? What was taking so long? Were Dagget and Crown just sitting waiting for an answer from Washington? Or had they taken off? Lyedekker would not have spoken his true thoughts to anyone. But deep inside he was beginning to have doubts. Maybe he'd bitten off more than he could handle. For all he knew Washington could be stringing him along. And maybe there was a troop of soldiers on its way here, to Hope. Hell, why did things have to be so damn complicated. When they'd boarded that train – expecting to walk off with a few wallets full of money – not even Lyedekker could have imagined their prize.

At first it had all seemed so simple. Take the passengers, inform Washington, and make his demands. It had been so easy. Too easy, now he considered the way things had seemed to be going. Hugo Lyedekker had lived too long in a hard world to allow himself to be lulled into thinking that things came easy. He knew different. But the hell of it was having to face the fact that his wild scheme, initially so foolproof, might yet blow up in his face. Lyedekker decided to hang on. It was too early in the game to quit yet. He might be running scared without cause. Why, right now, Dagget or Crown could be on the way to say that Washington had agreed terms. He grinned. By God, that would show 'em all! Show 'em that Hugo Lyedekker had more brains than a lot of folk gave him credit for. A childish chuckle of delight bubbled from his lips as he contemplated success. His doubts drifted away and Lyedekker found himself wondering just what he would do with all that money. Damn 'em all! He'd take it and run. Screw the goddam Government itself! And then live high on the hog and laugh in their faces.

The more he thought about it the more he liked the idea.

7

Angel picked up the abandoned spurline in the pale light of dawn. He rode in close, dismounted to take a look, and was able to see where bright metal showed through the rust of the tracks. A train had passed along the spurline recently. There were faint traces of soot here and there along the outer edges of the rails. The spurline cut away towards the north, up into the main bulk of the Maricopas, and that was the way Angel rode.

He trailed up into the silent reaches of the mountain, constantly aware of his vulnerability. A good man, armed with a rifle, would have little difficulty in picking him off from up there. It was a disquieting thought, and a man could have been forgiven for taking a dim view of such a situation. Frank Angel took it as simply another aspect of his profession. In his line of work he was constantly forced to expose himself to personal danger. He accepted the requirement without a fuss, though not lightly. Angel valued his life, valued it highly, and he would have been a fool not to be aware of the risks he took. But if he balked every time he saw potential danger he was no use to either himself or the Department. So he just carried on, seeing nothing exceptional in his behaviour. Many men were forced to work under such conditions, and did, and survived.

In the hour before noon he drew rein on a steep slope. He knew that Hope couldn't be far off now. For the last couple of hours he had been noticing the barely visible evidence of the old mine-workings. The slopes were dotted with yawning tunnel entrances, dried-out timberwork. At one or two of the larger sites lay exposed ore-trucks, overgrown by weeds, the metal red-rusty. The abandoned mines had a forlorn look to them. Deserted, silent, they remained as little more than the debris of human folly, the get-rich-quick fever that could ignite like a flame and spread just as quickly. And like a fast-burning flame the fever was apt to burn itself out too quickly, sputtering, then vanishing. The followers of the flame would move on, searching for a new place, leaving behind their forgotten dreams and dashed hopes.

After following the rail tracks Angel got his first look at the old town a couple of miles further on. The tracks stopped just short of the town. Hope itself, built in a shallow basin, couldn't have had much to offer during its short life, Angel decided. It was an ugly place, worse now in its state of neglect. A few roughly constructed buildings sprawled on either side of a rutted street. On the east side of the street the buildings had been constructed part-way up the slope of the basin itself. Crude cabins clung tenaciously to the rocky incline, worn paths zigzagging down to the basin floor.

Angel pulled his horse out of sight behind a weathered rock. He fished out his field glasses, found himself a comfortable spot and settled down. He began a systematic inspection of the town and the surrounding area. One of the first things he saw was the missing train. It stood at the end of the spurline and as far as Angel could see it was empty. Moving on to Hope itself Angel checked each building in turn. About midway along the street stood a two-storey building, its size and shape identifying it as a saloon-cum-hotel. A thin trail of smoke rose from a tilted chimney-pipe at the rear corner. Angel smiled to himself. Somebody was cooking lunch. He was about to check further on when a figure emerged from the saloon door, pausing on the sagging boardwalk to light a thin cigar. Angel focused in on the figure: a tall man with a long, sad face, a drooping mustache. Angel had seen the face before and had a name to go with it. Moss Kirby. The sorrowful features and lazy walk concealed a violent nature and a damn quick gun. A lot of men had been fooled by Kirby's benign appearance. Most of them were dead now. Kirby had once worn a badge and by all accounts had been a good lawman, but for some reason, known only to himself, Kirby had gone bad. Since the transformation he had done his best to reverse all the good established during his years as a lawman.

Kirby stepped down to the street, making his way along to the far end and then up the slope towards the cabins. Here he was joined by another man. This one carried a rifle. He gave all the signs of being on guard. Angel scanned the cabins. The only things worth guarding in this god-forsaken place would be a bunch of hostages! Angel studied the cabins closely. He couldn't see a thing. The windows were too dusty and he was too far away for even the field glasses to pick up anything.

Angel lowered the glasses, satisfied. At least he'd found the right place. All he had to do now was to get the hostages out. Getting here had been the easy part. From here on in he was going to have to work. He eased away from his vantage point, starting to turn.

And that was when he caught sight of a moving shadow on his right, sliding in towards him, silent, menacing.

For the first couple of seconds Angel carried on turning, as if he hadn't spotted the shadow. He placed the man by the size of the shadow and its position in relation to the sun. It gave him an approximate position. That was all he needed.

Twisting suddenly, without warning, Angel ducked in under the rifle butt swinging down at his skull. His body caught the man at knee-level, driving him back, bringing a surprised grunt from the man's throat. Then the man started to go down and Angel got his

61

feet under him, so that as the man hit the ground Angel was standing over him. The rifle slipped from the man's fingers as he struck the hard ground but he responded quickly, driving a boot-heel upwards at Angel's groin. Angel managed to jerk his body aside, catching the blow on his hip. It still hurt and there was enough force behind it to push Angel off his stride. As Angel side-stepped the man rolled to his feet, sledging a hard fist in a roundhouse punch that clouted the side of Angel's head. Pain flared wildly.

Angel set himself, easing back from a second punch, then leaned in and slugged the man hard, over the heart, following with a brutal left to the mouth. The man stumbled away from Angel, a surprised look in his eyes as he pawed at the blood pouring from his crushed lips.

While he was still hesitating Angel hit him again, this time using the hardened edge of his hand in a swift chopping motion. The blow struck with a solid sound. It had been delivered with terrible force and it snapped the man's collarbone as if it had been a rotten twig. The man went down on his knees, his face contorted with agony. He stared up at Angel as if he was some kind of monster too awful to look upon, not understanding how a mere man could have hurt him so much with nothing more than his hand. He felt the spreading flood of pain, swelling and rising, and it was too much to bear. There was only one thing he could do: what any animal will do when it is in pain, and he opened his mouth to scream.

Angel saw the scream coming, and knew he couldn't afford to allow any noise which might carry to the people down in Hope. He had to stop that scream. He did so swiftly. Mercilessly. With a single, powerful blow that utilized the same technique he had employed to put the man down. This time his palm edge came down across the back of the man's neck. The man's head sagged forward. There was a single, choked grunt of sound, and then the man flopped face down on the ground. He kicked in reflex a couple of times and then he was still. His outstretched left hand drew into a tight fist, opened, fingers splaying out on the hard ground, and then the man was dead.

Angel eased his Colt into his hand, checking the rocky slopes around him in case the dead man had a partner. He saw nothing. Heard nothing. After a couple of minutes he relaxed. He returned to where the body lay and turned it over. Lon Tucker had been the man's name, and he had been one of Lyedekker's bunch. That left three of them; Dagget was back at Fuller's Crossing, together with the man Angel had shot, Crown, now he had dealt with Tucker. So the remaining three would have to be Lyedekker himself, Moss Kirby, and Lyedekker's right hand man, Sam Huffaker. The worst of the bunch, Angel thought, or the best according to how you looked at it.

He moved to where his horse stood. Putting away the glasses Angel took his rifle, checked that it was fully loaded. Cutting away from his position he began to approach the town, gradually working his way in closer by a long, circuitous route which eventually brought him in at the south end. From here he was able to cross the spurline, moving swiftly along the sheltering bulk of the train and from there to the first of Hope's buildings. Crouched in the shadow of the end wall of what had been a large dry-goods store, Angel peered along the street. It was empty. He slipped round to the front of the store and stepped inside through a door hanging from one hinge.

As he had worked his way down from the high slope above the town an idea had germinated and blossomed in his mind. Angel had realized the need for some kind of diversion. Something to occupy Lyedekker and his men while Angel freed the hostages. Whatever that diversion was it had to be something capable of generating itself once Angel had set it in motion. The answer had proved to be childishly simple.

Angel decided to set Hope ablaze. It wouldn't take a deal of doing. The sun-bleached, tinder-dry wood was just begging for a spark. Once flames got a hold the whole place would ignite rapidly. It was a drastic scheme, but Angel saw no other way of creating his diversion.

He examined the store he was using for cover. Right here was as good a place as any, he thought. He gathered small oddments of loose debris, and took some dry paper off one of the empty shelves. With

64

these and a handful of splintered floorboarding Angel built a small pile of material against the store's long counter. He fished a match out of his pocket and scraped it alight, touching it to the screwed-up paper. Flames rose quickly, curling greedily against the dry wood, which in turn burst into crackling life. The rising flames spread up the side of the counter, along its length in either direction. Thick smoke began to roll up towards the rafters. Angel watched in silence, hoping that the flames wouldn't get a good hold before too much smoke showed outside the building. He needn't have worried. The open door and the broken windows allowed an access of air to be drawn into the building. There was a sudden whoosh of sound, like a hushed explosion, and flames burst across the room. The heat drove Angel out of the building. He took a chance and ran across the street, slipping into the shadow of a weed-choked alley. When he glanced across the street again the store was a mass of roiling flame, dense clouds of smoke pouring from the windows. Even as he watched part of the interior collapsed. Hot sparks drifted from the building. Flames began to reach out towards the next building.

Angel turned along the alley, emerging at the rear of the building. He began to work his way along the littered backlots, towards the cabins hugging the east slope of the basin. He could hear the roar of the fire behind him. Over the roofs he could see smoke drifting skywards, grey-white smudges against the brassy blue. Once he heard a man shout. Angel grinned, pleased with himself.

He broke free from the dirty backlots. The cabins lay above him. There wasn't a deal of cover for him on the slope. Angel didn't waste time bemoaning the fact. He made sure there was a bullet in the rifle's breech, set himself, and made a run at the incline.

The surface underfoot was loose and dusty. Angel had to concentrate on the job in hand, and it was because of that that he failed to see the tall figure of Moss Kirby straight away.

Angel could have ended up dead!

If it hadn't been for a slight mistake on Kirby's part he would have been. Instead of spotting his man and putting a bullet in him, Kirby allowed his anger to get the better of him. He had already seen the fire and the way it was spreading along the street, and then he'd seen Angel coming up the slope. Moss Kirby put two and two together and came up with an unpleasant answer. He realized that Angel and the fire went together. The fire was a diversion for Angel to get the hostages free. The conclusion confirmed Kirby's realization. Lyedekker's scheme had backfired. The law had found its way to the hideout. As far as Kirby knew there could be a whole damn posse behind this intruder. Then there was a chance he was on his own. Which didn't seem likely to Kirby. Either way, as he saw it, Lyedekker's plan was shot wide open. His demands were just so much crap. And everything had been for nothing! For sweet damn all! The whole shooting-match had been wasted. All the waiting. The back-breaking work clearing away the shit blocking the spurline. Guarding all those damn hostages. They'd been stuck out here in this godforsaken town for days . . . and for what?

Nothing!

And all of Moss Kirby's anger welled up in a moment of self-pity, expressed in a wild yell that was directed at the man on the slope.

'Sonofabitch . . . I've got one for you!'

Angel's head turned as he caught the hurled warning. He spotted Moss Kirby, saw the moving rifle in Kirby's hands and threw himself forward, belly down. He heard the sharp blast of the weapon, felt a hard tug at his left upper arm, and rolled, twisting frantically. Dust rose in a thin mist, stinging his eyes. Angel heard a second shot. He felt the impact as the bullet whacked the earth inches from him. He ignored the burning pain swelling across his arm, yanked his rifle round and triggered a swift shot in Kirby's direction. It was close enough to cause Kirby to break stride. It gave Angel precious seconds in which to get his feet under him, half-rising, jamming the rifle against one hip.

For what seemed a long time they faced each other, guns up and ready, a seeming reluctance to fire. It could have only been fleeting seconds, yet there was an unreal quality in the moment. Almost a suspension of movement, a long, drawn-out sigh that was destined to be broken. . . .

Angel's rifle blasted its sound across the stillness. A rapid volley of shots ripped into Moss Kirby, spinning him back, blood spraying from his broken body in a red mist, driving him back against the front of one of the cabins. Kirby dropped to his knees, his head lowered as if he was studying the gaping, bloody wounds in his body. He stayed that way as Angel crested the slope, moving towards him. Keeping a careful eye on Kirby, Angel kicked the man's rifle well out of reach, then plucked Kirby's handgun from its holster. It was then that Kirby slid over to one side, toppling face down in the dirt.

Angel moved along the line of cabins, checking each one. Then he heard the sound of someone banging on a door. Crossing to the cabin Angel found himself unable to hold back a wry grin. Somehow he just knew who was doing all the banging. Even thumping on a door the Attorney-General made his presence felt.

'Back off!' Angel yelled. He gave the cabin's occupants a few seconds to clear the door, then blew the lock apart with a couple of well-placed bullets.

The door swung open slowly and Angel watched as the Attorney-General and his companions filed out. They were a sorry bunch. The once-pressed and crisp suits were creased and stained, the white shirts soiled and sweaty. None of them had shaved for days, or washed, Angel thought, wrinkling his nose.

'At least you're consistent,' the Attorney-General grumbled as he joined Angel.

'Sir?' Angel asked.

The Attorney-General's steely gaze took in the flaming wreckage of the town. 'You managed to appear with your customary discretion!'

Angel ignored the sarcasm. He was busy fishing fresh shells from his pocket to feed into the rifle.

'At least the Department seems to be functioning in my absence,' the Attorney-General went on.

'Almost makes a man feel as if he's really needed,' Angel said very softly.

'Don't overstep the line, Mr Angel,' the Attorney-General warned. 'At least it has given me the opportunity of observing you in action. Brings a whole new light to bear on my past opinion of you.'

'Oh?'

'Yes. It confirms what I've thought for a long time!' the Attorney-General said and turned aside to gaze down on the scene below.

'Sir, where's Amabel?' Angel asked, a coldness forming in the pit of his stomach. The Attorney-General spun on his heel.

'My God! Here we are nattering away like old women! She's down there, Frank! In the saloon. Lyedekker took her down there after we'd attempted an unsuccessful escape.' The Attorney-General's features hardened. 'Lyedekker treated her pretty badly, Frank. He beat her in front of us all because of what she'd done!'

'Stay here,' Angel said, an edge to his voice. He indicated the dead Moss Kirby. 'Make use of his guns

69

if anybody tries to get near you. But stay here!'

The Attorney-General watched him go down the slope, realizing that nothing would deter Angel now. Telling Angel what he had was comparable with pulling the trigger of a gun. Once done there was no going back. Hugo Lyedekker was a marked man. Whether it happened now or in a year's time, Lyedekker would pay for what he had done to Amabel Rowe. And knowing Frank Angel the way he did, the Attorney-General had no doubt as to how Lyedekker would pay. For once, the Attorney-General thought to himself, Angel can handle it his own way with my approval. Unacknowledged, unspoken, and completely off the record, of course, he added in an attempt to appease the slight feeling of guilt he experienced.

8

'You were wrong!' Sam Huffaker yelled. 'Goddam you, Hugo, you were wrong! Now they've got us boxed in!'

'For Christ's sake, shut your mouth,' Lyedekker said, surprised at his own calmness. 'Before you start wettin' your pants, let's figure this out.'

Huffaker laughed shrilly. 'Ain't nothing to figure. The law's caught up with us an' we'll likely end up dead!'

'One man,' Lyedekker pointed out. 'That's all we seen.'

'Don't mean there ain't more of 'em!'

'Until I see 'em I ain't worrying,' Lyedekker said. He turned from where he was standing in the middle of the street and headed back inside the saloon. 'Sam, you go straight on through. Get the horses ready. We're heading out 'fore that son of a bitch up there comes lookin' for us!'

Huffaker paused on the boardwalk.

'You think we can make it?'

71

'Only way we'll find out is by doin' it. Now move your ass, Sam!'

As Huffaker left him Lyedekker took a final look over the town. Already flames were close to reaching the saloon. Thick smoke rose, blotting out the sun. Burning flakes of dry wood floated down, hovering in the hot, pulsing air. Lyedekker's earlier thoughts of success vanished. Washington had tricked him. Somehow they had got a man on their trail and now that man was tearing down the precarious scheme Lyedekker had built up. And if there was one man there could easily be more. Maybe they were just waiting for a signal. Well, I ain't, Lyedekker thought hotly. If the bastards want me they'll have to catch me first! He entered the saloon, crossing the littered room, pausing to snatch his rifle from a table. On the far side of the room he threw back the bolt on a door, kicked it open.

'Come on out, honey, time to go!'

Amabel Rowe stepped slowly from the small room, frowning slightly at his grinning expression.

'Go where?' she asked.

'You might say there's been a slight change in my plans, honey,' Lyedekker said. He reached out and took hold of Amabel's wrist. He dragged her along behind him as he skirted the far end of the long bar and went through to the rear of the saloon. On the other side of a storeroom a door stood ajar, exposing the overgrown backlot of the saloon.

'Mr Lyedekker, where are we going?' Amabel

asked as they emerged from the shadowed saloon into the hot, bright glare of the sun.

Lyedekker never once broke his stride. Over his shoulder he said:

'If this was the army, honey, this would be called a strategic retreat.'

'In your language, Mr Lyedekker, it translates as running away because the odds have changed.'

Lyedekker laughed. 'Pretty close, honey.'

They reached a low building standing off from the saloon's backlot. Sagging double doors stood open and Amabel could see the dim shapes of restless horses moving about inside.

'Move it, Sam!' Lyedekker yelled.

Sam Huffaker appeared, leading a pair of saddled horses. He took one look at Amabel and scowled.

'What the hell you brought her for?'

'Just a little insurance, Sam,' Lyedekker told him. 'The lady here's going to provide us with some protection. An' maybe even something to trade with if things get tight.'

'I don't know, Hugo,' Huffaker grumbled.

Lyedekker snatched the reins from Huffaker's hand.

'I do. So quit bellyachin' and bring another horse out here.'

Lyedekker glanced at Amabel who was watching him intently. He seemed amused by her expression, shaking his head at some private joke.

'I'm glad you find the situation funny, Mr

Lyedekker,' she remarked.

'And it ain't over yet,' Lyedekker said. 'Now get your pretty ass up in this here saddle, honey, an' don't get any notions about runnin' off, 'cause I promise if you do I'll shoot you full of holes.'

'I won't be much use as insurance if you kill me.'

'No, but it'll go a long way to satisfyin' me.'

Amabel struggled on to the horse, sitting uncomfortably in the hard saddle. She sat motionless, waiting for Lyedekker and Huffaker to ready themselves, and letting her mind wander. Was it Frank Angel out there? Was *he* this mystery stranger who seemed to be causing so much consternation? Had he, as the Attorney-General had hinted, somehow found his way here? And was he even now taking steps to free them from Lyedekker's control? Amabel had firsthand experience of the way Angel operated. She had seen him on assignment. Had in fact spent time with him in circumstances not unlike these. If there was a way Angel would find it, and he would not rest until he'd completed his task. He was extremely conscientious, she had found, in everything he did.

'Let's move, Sam,' Lyedekker snapped. He took hold of Amabel's reins and led her horse close beside his own as they eased around the end of the stable, cutting off towards the west. Lyedekker's intention was for them to slip away from Hope and lose themselves in the wilderness of rocky hills and canyons, the endless miles of emptiness.

'Jesus!'

Lyedekker's head came round at Huffaker's warning shout. He caught a quick glimpse of a running
figure closing on them fast, rifle in hands. Lyedekker
saw a tall man, lean, rangy, keen eyes in a face
burned brown from the sun. He was big, but he
moved easy, like an Indian, and Lyedekker was smart
enough to recognize a good man when he saw one.

'Sam, take the bastard!' Lyedekker yelled, clawing
for his holstered gun.

There was a flurry of movement at his side.
Amabel Rowe, her eyes blazing, threw herself across
Lyedekker's horse, slim hands reaching for his face.
He felt the sting of her nails raking his flesh, felt the
warm blood flow.

'You bitch!' He lashed out with a free hand, clout-
ing her across the side of the head. Amabel's slim
body went limp, hanging loosely across the front of
Lyedekker's saddle.

Lyedekker heard a single shot explode. He
glanced up and saw the running figure go down. He
figured him hit, but then he saw the man roll, twisting his body in a graceful curve. Lyedekker saw
Huffaker yanking his horse round, trying to line up
his gun for a second shot. Damn, Lyedekker thought,
he ain't going to make it! He pulled his own horse's
head round, ramming in his heels. The animal
lunged forward, closing on the man on the ground.
Lyedekker couldn't get his gun out in time. He drove
his horse at the the man, screaming his hate in a
cracked yell. He saw the man's attempt to leap aside,

felt the impact as his horse struck. The man fell away, cartwheeling across the hard ground, bouncing, slithering, coming to rest yards away, lying motionless.

Lyedekker hesitated, his hand on the butt of his gun. Then he spurred his horse on, following Huffaker's dusty trail away from Hope, and up into the granite peaks rearing over them.

9

'He's coming round!'

'Angel? Angel?' The voice drifted in from a long way off. Then: 'Frank, can you hear me?'

Angel opened his eyes. The Attorney-General was bent over him, concern mixed with impatience mirrored in his eyes.

'Pass me a cup of that coffee.' The Attorney-General's face vanished, only to reappear. 'And drink it,' he said. 'That's an order!'

Angel sat up slowly, testing his aching body. There was a numbness down his left side, and he recalled that that was the side the horse had struck. He took the cup of coffee the Attorney-General held out to him. Angel glanced around as he drank. They were on board the train. He was sitting on a leather couch in some plush Pullman coach. Angel stared out of the window. It was still daylight. He could see the smoking debris of the fire he'd started.

'How long have I been out?'

'Near enough an hour,' the Attorney-General told

him. 'How do you feel?'

Angel drained the cup of coffee. 'Give me another of those and I'll try and give you a report.'

Somebody brought him a refill. Angel recognized the man as a Supreme Court judge.

'They took Amabel with them,' Angel said bitterly.

'I know.' The Attorney-General stared out of the window. 'They rode west, up into the high country.'

'Lyedekker's no fool. He'll have figured he's lost this hand – but he won't quit the game.'

'And Amabel?'

Angel shrugged. 'Somebody he can use if he needs to bargain his way out of trouble. Lyedekker's the kind who likes every angle covered.'

The Attorney-General sighed. And then his mood changed abruptly.

'All right, my boy, we can handle things here now.'

Angel smiled thinly. In other words the Old Man was saying: you get up off your butt and go fetch that girl back safe and sound!

'I don't see the engineer or the fireman,' Angel said.

'You won't. They were killed just as soon as we arrived here. Lyedekker decided they were excess baggage.'

'We can still get out of this damn place, Charles,' cut in Orrin Whipple.

The Attorney-General glanced up at the Texan.

'I suppose you're going to tell me you can operate a locomotive.'

Whipple grinned. 'Hell, of course I can! Back when I was a boy I spent three years working on the railroad. Nothing fancy, mind, just a small company that used to run 'tween Laredo and San Antonio. But I did that trip four, five times a week.'

Angel climbed to his feet. 'I'll fetch my horse. Time I moved out.'

The Attorney-General followed him out of the coach.

'Just one thing,' Angel said. 'I had a run-in with some bounty hunters on the way in. They were set on taking Lyedekker for themselves. I warned them off but I got the feeling they weren't the sort who heeded warnings. There were three of them. Brothers by the name of Quint. Hard and mean, and there's only one way to deal with them.'

The Attorney-General nodded. 'I'll remember that. Keep it in mind yourself if you chance to meet up with them again.'

Angel raised a hand in a quick farewell and moved off, returning to where he'd left his horse. He mounted up and rode down into the basin, skirting the still-smoking ruins to come out at the place where Lyedekker and Huffaker had cut off towards the high country. It didn't take him long to pick up the trail. He still had most of the afternoon before him, and he figured to make good time before dark.

The trail led directly up into the high country. It was as if Lyedekker had a definite destination in mind. Or maybe he just intended to lose himself.

Find a place somewhere in the soaring heights where he could sit it out, wait until any pursuit had given up and gone home. Then he could make his choice and slip away unchallenged. There was no way Angel could know just which way Lyedekker was liable to jump. He couldn't read what was in the man's mind. All he could do was make a calculated guess and work on that.

Angel halted once, turning in the saddle to look down on Hope. He could make out the distant shape of the town. And moving away from a smudge of dark smoke was the thin, snakelike length of the train, gathering speed as it moved along the spurline. Well, Angel thought, at least that part of the job was over.

The higher he rode the rougher the way became. The slopes rose steeply above him, one moment bare rock and earth, the next loose drifts of shale. More than once he was forced to dismount, leading his horse across some tricky patch.

He was crossing a wide slope of shale, dividing his attention between watching where he was treading and keeping an eye on his nervous horse. There was no warning – just the impact of the bullet as it whacked the ground inches from him. Seconds later the sound of the shot reached him, echoing wildly back and forth. Angel instinctively glanced up. He caught a momentary glimpse of a rifle barrel reflecting the bright sunlight. Damn!

A second shot blasted a gout of earth up in his horse's face. The animal, already jumpy from crossing the loose shale, reared, shrilling its protest. Angel felt the reins drag against his hand. The horse felt itself sliding and thrashed in panic. Before Angel could free his hand from the reins the lunging horse went over on its side, pulling him with it. Angel desperately shook his hand free from the grip of the leather, though he was unable to stop himself falling. He slammed face down on the moving bed of shale, choking on the rising dust, and tried to halt his descent. Somewhere he could hear his horse scream-ing above the hissing rattle of stones. He went down maybe twenty feet before the slope levelled out a little, allowing him to claw himself to a stop.

Angel lay still. From his position he was able to see clear up to where he'd seen the rifle. He concen-trated on that spot now, only his eyes moving. Below him he could hear his horse grunting and panting in obvious pain. The sound tore at his nerves. Angel wanted to go to the animal but until he was certain the rifleman had gone he wasn't going to chance moving.

A long half-hour passed. The sun burned the back of Angel's neck. Sweat had soaked through his shirt and the material clung to his skin. Angel's eyes ached from staring up at the high place where the rifleman had concealed himself. He was beginning to figure he'd wasted enough time. There hadn't been a flicker of movement from up there. Not a solitary damn thing! Angel was as sure as he dared allow that the rifleman had gone. Lyedekker and Huffaker were the shoot-and-run type. It took the mentality of an Apache to put a man down then sit and wait for half a day to see if he really was dead. Which, Angel decided, was all supposition on his part, and he was going to look an awful fool if he stood up and had his head shot off!

Even so he wasn't going to lie out here on this damn slope, slowly broiling! Angel had always been willing to take a chance. You needed to be a gambler in his profession. He wished he had his rifle in his hands. His handgun wasn't going to reach that high spot. Angel could still hear his horse somewhere below him. If he could get down to it, get his rifle in his hands . . . maybe. . . .

Once he'd made up his mind he acted. There was nothing to be gained by just lying there thinking the matter over, working out a hundred reasons why he shouldn't move. It was one of the rules the Department training had hammered home. In any tricky situation take time to assess, then work out your strategy, then act on that decision. Don't hesitate. Don't wait too long, because you can be damn sure that the other feller isn't going to give you time!

Angel rolled over twice to the left, then drew his legs under him as he half-rose, arching his body over so that he went head first down the slope in a controlled dive. He struck on his shoulder, letting the natural impetus of his body carry him forward. In the fraction of a second before he'd hit Angel had seen his horse, some thirty feet further down the slope, on its side. He turned his body in that direction, turning and twisting as he slithered down the dusty shale. The animal's bulk brought him to a dead stop. Angel levered himself up and over the horse, slamming down on the far side, and lay gasping for breath, sweat streaming from every pore.

After a time he reached up and dragged his rifle from the scabbard. He levered a round into the breech and shuffled round until he could peer over the horse's bulk, up the long slope, to the place where the shots had come from.

Nothing.

No sound. No movement. Whoever had fired the shot was long gone. Angel stood up. He checked the entire surrounding area. Not a damn thing!

He looked the horse over. It had two broken legs and a long, deep gash in its neck. Angel removed what gear and supplies he needed, then took out one of the knives he carried in his boots. A shot from the rifle would have done the job just as efficiently, but the sound would have carried a long way. Angel wanted Lyedekker and Huffaker to think they were free from pursuit. He wanted them to get careless. Because if they became careless, casual, then he would be able to take them so much more easily.

He slung a canteen over his shoulder. His blanket-roll he carried on his back, hung on a light harness he'd made from sections of the rope coiled on his saddle. His belt-loops were full with extra loads for his guns. He took nothing else but a little dried beef and his canteen. Food was no problem. He could always find something to eat if the desire became too great to resist. As he started the climb up the shale slope he was chewing on a slice of dried beef.

Two hours later he was on his heels at the spot where the rifleman had waited for him. He found a half-smoked cigar and two empty bullet casings. After the shooting the rifleman had worked his way on foot back into the rocks. After casting around for a while Angel found where the man had left his horse. Faint tracks wound off into the higher slopes. After a time Angel came across the place where the rider had met up with a second horseman. The fresh tracks revealed that this animal was carrying double. Amabel? It had to be. Damn, Angel found himself thinking, it had to be!

He jerked his thoughts from her and moved on. The way underfoot now was getting rockier. Soon it would be all rock. And then there wouldn't be much sign left. The possibility didn't worry Angel too much. He would still be able to work out their line of travel. In this maze of tumbled rock there would only be a few places a horse could negotiate. A careful study of the terrain would show him where a horse could move and there were bound to be one or two small signs that he could spot. An iron horseshoe slipping on the rocky surface would leave a mark. Even the bulk of a horse rubbing against the side of a boulder could provide a marker in the form of a few hairs clinging to the rough surface. The men

Angel was following had already proved themselves to be careless. The tell-tale cigar butt. The used shell casings. It was likely that Lyedekker and Huffaker might leave a trail a blind man could follow.

Angel kept moving until full darkness forced him to stop. He found a sheltered place beneath tall boulders and unrolled his blankets. He finished off the last of the dried beef, allowed himself a little water, then wrapped himself in his blankets. He slept soundly, though lightly, and woke as first light spilled over the peaks above him. By the time the first rays of the sun warmed him he had been on the move for over an hour.

About mid-morning he came on the place where his quarry had camped for the night. Angel took a look around, searching for the cook-fire. He dug around in the ashes and judged that they must have been gone a couple of hours.

There was a dry creek running near where the camp had been sited and Angel picked up clear tracks moving along the sandy strip. After a couple of miles the creek curved off into a wide canyon that cut its way deep into the mountain. Angel followed the trail in.

If anything it was hotter in the canyon than out in the open. The heat lay trapped by the high canyon walls. It hung near the ground like a smothering blanket.

He was a half-mile into the canyon when he caught sight of movement on the far slope. It was at a place where natural erosion had broken the high cliff of the canyon wall. The wall had opened into what was practically a side canyon, offering entry and exit to the main channel. Three riders were coming down the dusty slope, breaking apart as they reached bottom, cutting across the open canyon floor, but all of them moving in Angel's direction.

He took one long look at them, recognizing them instantly, and knew he had trouble.

Luke! Charly! And Perce!

The Quint brothers!

And that could only mean one thing!

10

Angel dropped his canteen and blanket-roll and ran for the closest cover. He put the rifle to his hip, firing as he moved, because he knew damn well that the Quints hadn't come to pass the time of day. They'd come with the intention of burying him!

Perce was the closest and he opened fire without even bothering to take aim. His shots came in a steady stream, slapping the ground around Angel, none coming close. Perce wasn't allowing for the fact that he was in the saddle of a fast-moving horse, and it showed in the way his bullets hit.

Angel saw that he wasn't going to reach cover before Perce got to him so he stopped, turning sideways on, presenting Perce with a smaller target. He put the rifle to his shoulder and shot Perce's horse from beneath him. Perce felt the horse going down and kicked his feet free from the stirrups. As his horse dropped from under him Perce was flung clear. He hit the ground hard, slithering helplessly, losing his grip on his own rifle.

There was a shrill protest of sound from Charly Quint's horse as he savagely yanked the reins round, turning the horse in mid-stride. There was an ugly look on Charly's face as he drove in his heels. He threw himself from the saddle as he neared Perce, yanking a heavy revolver from his belt. Standing over Perce he snapped off a couple of shots in Angel's direction.

Angel felt the wind from one bullet. He pulled back, dragging the muzzle of his rifle round. He heard the slam of sound from Charly's revolver again, and this time something burned across the muscle of his left arm. In the same moment Angel's finger touched the trigger and his rifle blasted out a single shot.

Charly Quint let out a high scream as the bullet took him in the chest. It kicked him off his feet and put him on the ground. Charly lay writhing in agony, his body twisting in a macabre dance of death. Blood was pumping from the hole in his chest and when he began to cough it gouted from his mouth.

Angel didn't waste time watching. The moment he'd fired at Charly he turned and ran for a shallow depression in the earth. It was only yards away, but with the thunder of Luke Quint's horse racketing in his ears it seemed a lifetime away. Angel was still a couple of yards short when he threw himself forward in a desperate dive. He could almost feel the hot breath of Luke's horse on the back of his neck. As he dropped over the lip of the depression, twisting his body, Angel sensed the looming bulk of Luke's horse. He smashed to the hard ground, grunting in response to the battering his body received. Dust and flinty pebbles rained down on him as Luke's horse thundered across the depression, its hoofs inches above him. Angel squirmed round, thrust his rifle forward, triggered a hasty shot at Luke Quint and missed.

There was a stillness. An uneasy quiet. Luke Quint had taken his horse out of range. Angel watched him for a moment, then turned to where Charly Quint lay still and silent. But Perce was far from still or silent.

'Hey! You son of a bitch! You killed Charly!'

Perce was on his feet. He had his gun in his hand and he was walking in Angel's direction.

'You hear me? Mister son of a bitchin' Justice Department man! Stand up an' let me see your goddam face!'

Go to hell, you bastard! Angel mouthed the words silently as he laid the rifle across the edge of the depression, sighting in on the advancing Perce.

'You goin' to show yourself, boy?' Perce demanded.

There was no answer. Perce Quint scowled angrily. He flipped the handgun in the direction of the depression and pulled the trigger, fired again. The bullets whacked the earth on the edge of the depression.

'Bet you heard that!' Perce yelled. He looked beyond the depression to where his brother Luke sat his horse. 'Come on, Luke, we got the bastard between us! Let's take him!'

Angel had the same thought in mind. That he was between two guns. Caught in the middle. He didn't find the idea appealing.

'Now, Luke, now!' Perce screamed, and lunged forward.

Angel heard the drum of hoofs at his rear. That meant Luke was making his play. Angel snapped the rifle to his shoulder and fired. The bullet took Perce on the run, spinning him off his feet. Perce slithered forward, on his knees, his face twisted in pain. Blood started to spread across the front of his shirt. Even then Perce managed to loose off another shot. By a supreme effort he stayed on his knees, determined not to go down. Angel, knowing that Luke was closing on him fast, realized he had to take Perce out. He put a bullet through Perce's head, then twisted over on his back to face the oncoming Luke.

The man was closer than Angel had anticipated. Luke's gunhand was chopping down, the long barrel of the revolver spitting a gout of flame. The bullet chunked into the earth beside Angel. Luke was pulling the trigger for a second shot when Angel fired. He saw Luke arch back in his saddle, a splash of blood marking the front of his dirty buckskin shirt. And then something struck him a powerful blow on the left side of his body, just below the ribs. The impact drove the breath from his body. Angel gasped out loud against the stunning pain. He fought to keep control of his senses, turning as Luke's horse raced on by him. Angel tried to lift his rifle but it had grown heavy and awkward in his fingers. He let it drop and snatched his Colt from the holster. By the time he had it levelled Luke Quint was out of range. Luke was hunched over in his saddle, swaying slightly as his horse carried off down the canyon and out of sight.

The scene in front of Angel blurred. He let the Colt rest on the ground as a great weariness swept over him. Reaching down he explored the place where Luke's bullet had struck. He felt the slick warmth of flowing blood and for a second a sensation of panic rolled over him, a coldness gripping his insides. But then his instinct for survival took over. You caught a bullet, Frank, he told himself, but it isn't the first time. It hasn't killed you yet so there's a chance it won't if you treat it right.

He glanced about him. He could see the horse he'd shot from under Perce Quint. Behind the saddle were saddlebags and other gear. A big canteen hung from the saddle itself. All right, Frank, my boy, all you have to do is walk over there and get what you want. A thin smile touched his lips. It sounded so damned easy when he said it. The doing was a lot harder.

It took him a while to climb to his feet. He kept his left hand pressed tightly over the wound. The Colt dangled from his right. He took it step by step, pausing often to catch his breath. He was angry at himself for his weakness, though he knew it was only his body reacting to the shock of the bullet. He seemed to walk for ever.

The distance never lessened. Once he stumbled, his legs seeming to drift away from his body. The jolt as he fell to his knees brought a burst of raw pain. It flared like a silent explosion, racing through his body, dragging a low moan from his lips. Sweat beaded his face. Angel stared through the haze before his eyes, willing the dead horse to stay just where it was. He was sure the damn thing was moving! He climbed awkwardly to his feet and staggered forward. Now he didn't judge distance or time. He simply kept walking, and the next thing he knew he was damn near tripping over the dead horse.

He loosened the saddlebags with thick, clumsy fingers. Dragged them clear. He unhooked the canteen. In the other bundle of gear he found cooking untensils and food. Angel gathered the stuff together and draped it across his shoulder, picked up his gun and went looking for a place to hide himself away. He managed to recover his own discarded canteen and blanket-roll, picking up his rifle as he passed the place where he'd made his stand.

Even later, when he had time to sit back and reflect on that time, Angel was never able to get a clear picture of what happened back in the canyon. His recall only allowed him to remember the beginning. How he had stumbled off, searching for a hidden place, somewhere where he could secrete himself and look to his wound. The rest was a time-less blur, a formless picture full of shadows, tinged with pain and a dim knowledge that he had to keep himself alive.

Like some injured animal he had walked and crawled and stumbled his way along the canyon, eventually searching out a narrow side-canyon that burrowed deep into the sheer walls. It was a place of deep shadow, seeing little sunlight, the twisting floor littered with debris. Further along there was a mass of tumbled, splintered rock and beyond that a place where the canyon widened out into a dead-end. In the far corner water bubbled up from some under-ground source, flowing into a shallow pool. A little grass grew along the edges of the pool. Angel crawled the last few yards, dumped his gear, and plunged his fevered face into the cool water.

Time drifted. During the long, slow hours of the afternoon he had roused himself. Pain from the wound gnawed at his insides like some living crea-ture. He sat up and took off his shirt. Where the blood had congealed around the wound the material clung to his skin. Angel knew he wouldn't get the shirt off without making the wound bleed again. He opened the saddlebags he'd taken from Perce Quint's horse and tipped the contents on the ground beside him. He found a grubby bandanna. Angel washed it out in the pool, then rinsed it, wadded it up and held it against the dried, caked blood.

He had to repeat the operation a number of times

before the water loosened the dry blood and allowed him to ease the shirt away from the wound. The bullet hole was neat and round, slightly swollen and bruised around the edges. Angel prodded it with careful fingers. It was sore. He knew that the bullet was still in there somewhere. The main source of pain was centered in the region of his stomach. From what Angel could judge the bullet must have entered at an angle, going in on his left side, then driving into the hard, ridged stomach muscles. It hadn't gone deeper. He was sure of that. If it had he would have been in a lot more pain. The bullet must be lodged in the tough layer of muscle over his stomach, he figured, and he thanked the long, gruelling hours he put in at the Department's gym. The punishing exercises, the brutal sessions with Kee Lai, the martial-arts instructor. Once again he was in the Korean's debt.

Angel searched through the stuff he'd emptied from the saddlebags. In a roll of cloth he found a quart bottle of whiskey. It was good quality too, not some backwoods brew conjured up by a moonshiner. Angel pulled the cork and took a long swallow. The liquor burned all the way down to the tips of his toes and brought tears to his eyes. He used a good third of the bottle on the wound, pouring it liberally into the hole. It burned like hell on a busy day, and Angel swore with all the fluency of an Irish trooper. He just hoped that the sacrifice was warranted. It was a shame to use good whiskey in such a way but Angel figured that his outsides needed it more than his insides.

Afterwards he fashioned a pad from the bandanna and bound it in place with strips of material cut from a shirt he found amongst Perce Quint's belongings. There wasn't much else he could do. The bullet would have to stay where it was until he had the time to go looking for a doctor. Angel pulled his shirt back on, and before he did anything else he looked to his guns, reloading them and placing them close at hand.

He dragged the canvas bag containing cooking-gear to his side. There was food, a tin containing coffee, cups and plates, coffee-pot and a battered frying-pan. At the bottom of the bag was a large bundle wrapped in oilskin. Angel opened it and saw that it contained dry buffalo droppings. Whatever the Quints might have lacked, they certainly knew the art of surviving in rough, barren country. Angel built a small fire with the dry chips, using one of his few remaining matches to get it started. It took a long time but eventually he was able to sit back and devour a plate of beans and a thick slice of tough, chewy bacon. There was a full pot of strong coffee bubbling on the fire. Angel drank the lot, spicing it with the remains of the whiskey.

It was starting to get dark by then. Angel put out the fire, dragged his blankets over him, and slept. There was nothing else he could do. If he had succeeded in keeping himself alive this long, then rest would keep him on the right road. His body would take over his recovery. It would be gradual and he would be weak for some while. But Angel knew that he would live. He was young and fit and he had great reserves of strength; his body would draw on those reserves now. All he could do was to wait.

He woke to the warmth of sunlight on his face. Angel opened his eyes and blinked against the glare. High overhead, above the sheer walls of rock, was a patch of blue sky. The sun hung directly over him, and Angel realized that he had slept through the morning. He eased the blankets from him and sat up slowly, testing his reactions. He was stiff, his body aching from a long night on the hard ground. There was a dull ache in the region of the wound. Not sharp pain: just a nagging, pulsing ache. Angel probed the wound. It was still sore but no more than it had been the day before. He sat for a while, then risked climbing to his feet.

It was only when he rose that he found how weak he still was. He stood with all the grace of a newborn colt, legs trembling, splayed wide apart to keep his balance. When he looked up the rock walls around him spun and a giddy sickness welled up. Angel took a couple of steps and leaned himself against the rock-face at his back. He stayed there until the sensation passed. He touched his face, feeling the sweat beading his skin. His hand moved down to his lower jaw and he felt the itchy stubble. If he looked as bad as he felt, he thought, then he wouldn't need a gun –

he'd frighten a potential adversary away!

He was wrong. He was going to need his gun much sooner than he expected

Much sooner.

11

'You comin' out, boy, or do I have to come in and get you?'

Angel sat up, reaching for his gun. He rose from his blankets and moved to the far side of the canyon. It was almost fully dark, the black shadows filling the canyon. Angel pressed himself against the hard, cold rock and waited.

He knew who it was out there, beyond the tumbled barrier of stone: Luke Quint. Angel's bullet hadn't been enough to kill him. Luke must have been wandering around out in the main canyon, maybe delirious, hurt, but fired with enough hate to keep him on his feet. And now he had found Angel's hiding-place. Luke had come for his revenge.

'Son of a bitch!' Luke grumbled. There was a sharp clatter of tumbling rock. 'Damn!' Then: 'I know you're in there! Boy, I aim to kill you this time! Why don't you come on out here? I'm goin' to get you anyhow . . . You listenin' to me, you bastard?'

Angel was listening all right. But he wasn't about

to answer. Luke could do all the yelling he wanted. Angel was content to wait for the man to show himself, then he'd let his gun do his talking.

'Boy, I'm on my way! An' this time'll finish it! Twice you put bullets in me, boy, but I ain't dead yet! You done for Charly an' ol' Perce right enough. Shit, you asshole, I ain't about to roll over for you!'

The soft sound of a heavy body easing across the pile of rock reached Angel's ears. He saw a humped shape rise above the ridge of rock, then roll down the uneven surface. A few dislodged stones rattled as they fell. Angel eared back the Colt's hammer, peering into the gloom. He made out a dark shape, crouching at the foot of the rocks. The figure remained motionless, save for the head.

Angel took a short step back to give himself room to move. The sleeve of his shirt brushed the rock at his side. It was a tiny, hushed fragment of sound, but it was more than enough for someone like Luke Quint.

The crouched figure turned, rose upright, lunged forward. There was a wink of orange flame followed by the thunderous crash of a shot. The bullet smashed against the rock, splinters of stone stinging Angel's face. The sharp needles of pain jerked him into a response. Angel fired as he moved, ducking low, firing again. Winking spears of flame illuminated the darkness.

'Son of a bitch, I got you this time!' Luke Quint yelled.

Angel smiled to himself. The man was a fool. He couldn't have advertised his position better with a lighted lamp. His voice told Angel just where he was. He sank down on one knee, steadying the Colt two-handed, and put two quick bullets into Luke Quint.

Luke grunted in surprise as the bullets hammered his chest. The force behind them shoved him off balance and he fell hard, twisting over on to his stomach. He tried to get up, coughing, felt blood rise in his throat. His legs wouldn't support him and he plunged forward, falling head first into the pool with a heavy splash.

After a long time Angel climbed stiffly to his feet. He crossed over to where Luke Quint lay and dragged the body clear of the pool, rolling it out of sight against the base of the canyon wall. He stared down at Luke Quint for a time. What a damn waste, he thought. Three men dead, and for what? A couple of thousand dollars! They must have wanted that bounty pretty bad. He put away his gun, thinking: but not badly enough!

Angel gathered together the gear he needed. He climbed the pile of rock and made his way along the dark canyon until he reached the place where it joined the main canyon. Luke Quint's horse was there. It raised its head and stared at Angel. He went to it, talking quietly. A few minutes later he was in the saddle and moving off along the canyon.

Two hours later he reached the far end of the canyon. It opened out on a wide slope of the mountain. Angel knew he was going to have to wait until daylight before he could pick up Lyedekker's trail again. He chose a spot and settled down for the night, finding it hard to sleep. He'd lost time back in the canyon. More time than he dared admit.

It took him almost an hour to pick up the trail. Full light was on him by the time he put his horse down the slope, pushing it as hard as he dared. The trail still led west, but Angel noticed that he was leaving the high country behind. Gradually he was moving down through the mountain slopes. Had Lyedekker changed his mind? If so, where was he going now? Angel sighed. Speculation would result in nothing more positive than a headache. He settled back in his saddle and prepared to follow the faint trail. It was bound to end somewhere, sooner or later.

12

The marshal of Trinity was a short, moon-faced man with soft bags beneath his eyes and a greying moustache that drooped below his chin. His name was Milt Barnes. He was forty-eight years old and was the first to admit a liking for the peaceful life. He stood with Frank Angel in the small office of the town jail, scratching the back of his neck, trying to think of something to say to the grim, travel-stained man who had identified himself as an investigator for the Justice Department from Washington.

'So you think they might have been through here?' Angel asked again. He was having a hard time keeping control of his impatience. Barnes was a slow talker, deliberating before he put thoughts into words.

'Wish I could be more certain, Mr Angel,' Barnes said. 'All I can tell you is what Fabianni told me. Couple of nights back this feller come into his store. Round eight o'clock. Bought a pile of supplies. Some ammunition. And some clothing. Fabianni didn't pay too much attention to the man. He was getting ready to close and all, so he just served him and locked up after the feller left.'

'But he thinks he saw another rider with a young woman?'

Barnes nodded. 'While he was closing the door he saw the man he'd served mount up and ride down the street. Near the livery the man stopped and waited and this other rider showed. He must have been in the alley. They joined up and rode off. The second rider had this woman sitting behind him. Fabianni said she had fair hair.'

It sounded conclusive. And it made Angel's job that much easier. If Lyedekker and company stayed near civilization, in any form, then they were going to be seen. Which was going to help.

'Marshal, you got a doctor in town?' Angel asked.

Barnes nodded. 'Sure. Doc Franklin. He's a good man.'

'Get him,' Angel said. 'I'm going over to the telegraph office. I'll be there for a while. Can you bring the doc over?'

'Sure, Mr Angel, whatever you say.'

They left the office together. Angel cut across the dusty street, making for the telegraph office. Beyond the buildings he could see the dull gleam of the Gila River. The water was slow-moving, almost sluggish. It was a description which fitted the town of Trinity like the proverbial glove.

The telegraph office was a bare, weathered building stuck between a hat-shop on one side and a drapery on the other. Angel shoved open the creaky door and went in. Bright sunlight, streaming in through the dusty windows, laid pale shafts of yellow on the scuffed floorboards.

'Help you?' the telegraph operator asked. He was a skinny young man with steel spectacles perched at the tip of his thin nose. A green eyeshade was pulled level with the spectacles.

Angel tossed his badge on the counter and let the man read it.

'I want a priority clearance all the way through to the Department of Justice in Washington,' Angel told him. The man's eyes glittered.

'Yessir,' he said, and almost ran to his key.

Marshal Barnes arrived with the doctor while the clearance was being organized. Franklin was an experienced medic who had weaned himself on gunshot wounds. He examined Angel efficiently, nodding to himself as he studied the wound.

'Well, she's in there all right, Mr Angel,' he said. 'It giving you much pain?'

'Some,' Angel said. He glanced at the doctor. 'What happens if you take it out now?'

Franklin's eyebrows lifted. 'If?'

'Yeah,' Angel said. 'Look, Doc, I've got things to do and places to go, and none of 'em can wait. If taking that bullet out means I'm going to have to sit back and rest then we forget it.'

'Figure you're tough do you?' Franklin asked.

'I don't figure, Doc, I know,' Angel said evenly, and there was no arrogance in his tone. Simply the matter-of-fact way a man might say I'm white or I'm black. Franklin eyed the young man before him and decided that if anyone knew what he was talking about, then Frank Angel did. Franklin hadn't failed to notice the healed scars marking Angel's body.

'All right,' he said. 'Fasten your shirt, hardcase, and listen to some advice, from an older and wiser man.'

Angel drew a message pad to him and started to write down the first section of his report.

'Go ahead, Doc, I'm listening.'

'Whatever it is you have to do, Angel, get it done fast and then get that bullet out. I don't think you're in immediate danger but there's no telling with something like this. I've known men carry a piece of lead round with them all their lives and they never had a minute's trouble. But it works the other way too. Man gets shot. The bullet stays in and he feels fine. He carries on with his life. Two years later that bullet has worked its way deep enough to puncture his heart. That, Mr Angel, is pure medical fact. I can vouch for it because I was the one who cut the body open and found the bullet. It had travelled over four inches inside his body.'

Angel finished writing. He shoved the pad across the counter to the operator.

'Soon as you get through send that,' he said. Then he turned to Franklin. 'I get the message, Doc, and thanks. And I won't forget. Minute I'm free I'll have it seen to. Anything I can do in the meantime?'

'You need anything for the pain?'

Angel shook his head. 'It's bearable. Anyhow, it reminds me to be careful.'

Franklin smiled. 'Is it any use me saying don't do anything too strenuous?'

'Hell, Doc, you can say it.'

'I figured as much.' Franklin made for the door. 'If you need me for anything, Angel, my office is up the street.'

'Thanks, Doc.'

Franklin nodded. 'Good luck.'

'What can I do to help?' Marshal Barnes asked.

'Arrange for a fresh horse and have it saddled. See to it there are plenty of supplies. No way of knowing where I might end up or how far from the nearest town.'

Barnes nodded and hurried out of the office. There was a sudden chatter of sound from the telegraph.

'She's all clear,' the operator said. He placed Angel's message before him and began to transmit. Angel watched for a minute, then went and sat down. From past experience he knew he was in for a long session.

By the time he left the telegraph office Angel was feeling hungry enough to eat a bear – fur, claws and all. He made his way along the street until he saw what he was looking for. Inside the restaurant he found himself a table by the window and ordered himself a steak with all the trimmings.

Marshal Barnes came into the restaurant as Angel was finishing his meal. He was red-faced and sweating.

'Wait 'til you hear this,' he panted.

Angel drained his cup of coffee and waited.

'Herb Greer just rode in. He owns a small spread about a day's ride to the west. Early yesterday he had visitors. They took three of his horses and shot Billy Jenks, the feller who rides for Greer.'

'Lyedekker?' Angel asked.

'Seems most likely,' Barnes said. 'Greer said there were two men and a young woman. The woman was riding double with one of the men, an' Greer says from what he could see, the woman wasn't too happy bein' with the men.'

Angel got up. He placed some money on the table and followed Barnes out of the restaurant. They crossed the street and went straight into the jail. The man called Greer was there. He stood up as Angel and Barnes entered the office. Greer was a tall, lath-thin man, burned a deep brown. When he took off his hat he revealed thinning, sandy hair.

'Did the men say anything between themselves?' Angel asked. 'About where they might be heading?'

'No, sir,' Greer said. 'They didn't say much at all. Just told me to run out the horses, change the saddles and stuff. Then they had me find a saddle for the third horse. For the lady. That was it.'

'The girl,' Angel asked. 'How was she?'

'She looked like she'd been having a rough time. I mean, it was hard to tell. She was pretty dirtied up, but somebody had given her face some bruises. Made me mad as hell to see it. Under all that dirt she looked a right pretty thing.'

'She is,' Angel found himself saying.

Greer glanced at him closely. 'You know her, mister?'

'I know her.'

'Hell, I wish I could tell you more, then. Maybe if I'd got to town sooner. But I had to tend Billy. Thought he was going to pull through at first but he took a bad turn.' Greer swore bitterly. 'Weren't no need for him to die! Those bastards had no reason to kill him!'

'Mr Greer, they don't need reasons,' Angel said. 'Just one thing. Which way did they ride out?'

'West,' Greer said.

'What's out that way?'

Greer shrugged. 'Nothing much. Once they get the far side of my range there ain't a deal. Pretty rough country out there. Desert and the like. If they keep on going they'll reach California. But there's a deal of hard country before that.'

'Thanks, Mr Greer,' Angel said. He nodded to Marshal Barnes. 'That horse ready for me?'

'Yessir,' Barnes said. 'Down at the livery. All saddled up and ready to go. I seen to it you got enough supplies to last you a week, and I put on two big canteens of water.'

'Sounds like I'm going to need them. Thanks for your help, Marshal, I'm obliged.'

Angel left the office and made his way to the livery stable. The horse Barnes had picked for him was a powerful black. It looked like the kind of horse that would just keep on going. Angel took the reins from the liveryman, swung into the saddle and touched the black's sides. The horse moved off instantly and Angel could sense its desire to run.

He picked up the tracks Greer had made on his trip into town. Angel put the black to a steady run. First to the Greer ranch, then pick up the trail left by the three riders going west. After that? It was anybody's guess. Or would it be so difficult? Angel wondered about that. Lyedekker seemed to have a thing about moving west. Maybe his ultimate destination *was* California. It was a big piece of territory and there were plenty of places for a man to hide. At the southern end was Baja California, which was even more desolate. There was San Francisco. A man could lose himself easily in that sprawling city.

For some odd reason Angel found himself thinking about Amabel. He had forced her as far to the back of his mind as he'd been able. Things were difficult enough at the present without letting himself worry over her constantly. She was always there, but so far he had been able to control his concern for her. Now, though, she rose to the forefront of his thoughts, and with an almost paternal concern he felt all the old fears for her safety rise up. It was a bit crazy. He found that he was becoming a little frantic over her. He couldn't explain it. The feeling manifested itself and remained. Angel didn't fight it. He concentrated on the ride, and gradually the feeling subsided, drifting to the back of his mind again. But Angel knew that he wasn't going to be able to dismiss Amabel from his thoughts completely. Not now.

13

Lyedekker's plan didn't appeal to Huffaker all that much. But he couldn't deny that they needed the money. With grudging reluctance he agreed to go along with the scheme, and they finalized it as they sat eating breakfast at the spot where they had chosen to make camp.

'One thing I got to get straight,' Huffaker said. He jabbed a finger in Amabel Rowe's direction. 'What about her?'

Amabel gave him a scathing look.

'Don't worry about me,' she said. 'I'm going to wait outside the bank and hold the horses!'

Lyedekker roared with laughter. 'Sam, it's time you learned not to try and out-talk our Amabel. Hell, boy, she was the Attorney-General's own private secretary, an' that's a job needs brains!'

'Yeah?' Huffaker wasn't impressed. 'Far as I'm concerned she's just another female. Good for only one thing!'

'Mr Huffaker, with a mind as low as yours I'm

surprised you have the intelligence to stand up and walk!' Amabel retorted coldly.

Huffaker's face flushed, and he began to get up, knocking over his mug of coffee.

'Bitch!' he snapped. 'Time somebody showed you—'

Reaching out Lyedekker grabbed Huffaker's arm and held him firm. 'Just ease off, Sam,' he said. 'Ain't nobody about to touch her but me.'

'Damn smartmouth bitch!' Huffaker grumbled. He shot a sly glance at Lyedekker. 'Maybe it's time you slipped it to her, Hugo! Too much thinking ain't good for a woman. She needs somethin' to take her mind off all them fancy ideas.'

Lyedekker smiled across at Amabel

'That right, honey? That what you really need?'

'You think what you like, Mr Lyedekker,' Amabel said. 'But keep it to yourself. Don't try anything because it just wouldn't be worth it.'

'Hell, man, that's fightin' talk!' Huffaker grinned. He punched Lyedekker's arm. 'Nothin' better than a frisky filly, Hugo!'

Lyedekker just smiled. 'We'll see, pretty lady. There'll be a time and a place. Then we'll see.'

They broke camp a while later, mounted up and began the ride down out of the sandstone hills to the town of Paxton. It was an average-sized place, sited close to a shallow creek, and existing by the courtesy of the outlying ranches. It boasted four saloons, a couple of brothels, and a small, whitewashed adobe mission. It also had a stone-built jail and a bank constructed of similar material. As far as Hugo Lyedekker was concerned the saloons and the brothels didn't count, the jail was a damn eyesore, but the bank was the most interesting building in town. He had visited Paxton the night before, taking a quiet drink, then a casual stroll along the street, passing the bank on his return. It told him all he needed to know.

It was around ten-thirty when they rode in along Paxton's dusty main street. Lyedekker led the way to the bank and they reined in at the hitch rail. Easing his bulk in his saddle Lyedekker glanced across at Amabel.

'You remember what I said. Just do like I say. Try any funny business and I'll start shooting at the first person I see. And like I said, honey, if you don't think I'll do it, you go right ahead and yell.'

'I won't give you any trouble, Mr Lyedekker,' Amabel said. She knew very well that he meant what he said. If she caused any problems he would kill innocent people. Amabel couldn't have lived with that on her conscience, and Hugo Lyedekker knew it.

They dismounted slowly and tied the horses. Nobody gave them a second glance. Lyedekker took the lead, Huffaker at the rear, with Amabel between them. At the door to the bank Lyedekker glanced easily over his shoulder.

'Just do like I say, honey. Nothing else.'

As they stepped inside Huffaker eased the door shut. There were three people behind the cashiers' counter and two customers.

'Honey, you stand aside now,' Lyedekker said as he slipped his gun into his hand. Out of the corner of his eye he saw Huffaker do the same as Amabel moved away from them.

'All set, Sam?' Lyedekker asked. Huffaker nodded, and Lyedekker put up his gun.

'Everybody just stay where you are! Hands in plain sight! This ain't no trick or treat!'

There was a general gasp as Lyedekker's words sank home. All eyes swivelled to look in Lyedekker's direction, noted the levelled guns, then everybody did as they were told. Behind the counter one of the cashiers, a white-faced young girl, began a terrified scream. Lyedekker saw it coming and thrust his gun in the girl's direction.

'You do that, honey, and I'm going to shut you up in a way that'll make one hell of a mess.' Lyedekker's tone convinced the girl and she choked off the scream hurriedly. 'You,' he said to a stern-faced man behind the counter. 'If you're the boss-man get some bags and fill 'em. Paper money's all I want. No damn coin.' As the man moved to obey Lyedekker glanced across at Huffaker. 'Keep an eye on the outside, Sam. Don't want any damn fool walkin' in and raisin' a fuss.'

Behind the counter the man held up a bulging canvas bag. He placed it in front of Lyedekker, then

114

moved to fill a second bag.

'Move your ass, you son of a bitch!' Lyedekker snapped. 'We ain't got all day!'

The man nodded and scooped crumpled banknotes into the bag. He moved to place the second bag beside the first. A slow smile was easing across Lyedekker's face. The man seemed to return the smile, then he hesitated, his left hand below the level of the counter. Something in his expression warned Lyedekker, and he was already pulling the trigger of his gun as the man yanked his left hand into view, thrusting a short-barrelled revolver across the counter. Lyedekker's gun blasted out its heavy sound and the bullet crashed into the man's chest, flinging him back against the far wall. Blood welled from the black hole in his shirt, spreading rapidly as the man slithered helplessly to the floor.

'Goddam it to hell!' Lyedekker roared. He snatched up the two bags of money and while Huffaker threw open the door, Lyedekker waved his gun in Amabel's direction. 'After you, honey!'

They emerged on to the boardwalk, and found themselves facing chaos. People were running in every direction, and a lot of them were making for the bank. Lyedekker swore angrily as he spotted a fair number of drawn guns.

'Christ, Hugo!' Huffaker said.

'Quit griping and get the damn horses!' Lyedekker screamed. He yanked his gun into position and fired twice. His first bullet kicked up dirt, but his second hit a running man in the stomach, slapping him to the ground in a screaming heap. The effect on the other men was startling. They broke apart, seeking cover, and Lyedekker laughed. 'Goddam yeller-bellies!'

'Hugo!' Huffaker's plea almost went unheard. He was struggling to control the horses. The shooting had unnerved them and Huffaker was having a hard time freeing the reins. 'For God's sake!'

A rifle shot crashed out. The bullet chewed a long splinter of wood from the boardwalk close to Lyedekker's left boot.

'Throw the guns down! And I mean now!'

Lyedekker glanced up and saw a tall, grim-faced man walking steadily across the street. The man wore a dark suit and hat, and he had a badge pinned to the front of his vest. He had a revolver strapped to his waist and carried a rifle in his hands.

'You hear me? This is Marshal Culhane, and I suggest you do what I say right quick!'

'Damn fool!' Lyedekker said, his voice so low that only Amabel heard it. 'Man who talks like that only gets what he deserves!' And as he spoke he levelled his gun, putting two shots through the marshal's chest. Culhane gave a stunned cry, stumbling sideways, then flopped face down in the street, his blood staining the dusty ground. 'Sam, my rifle!'

Huffaker snatched Lyedekker's rifle from the sheath and tossed it to him. Lyedekker levered a

116

round into the chamber and began to fire on anyone who dared to show their face.

But despite the outlaws' shock attack, the citizens of Paxton resisted. A number of guns opened up, bullets burning the air around Lyedekker and Amabel and Huffaker. One of them hit Lyedekker's horse and it screamed in agony, thrashing wildly. Huffaker was almost knocked off his feet. He whirled about, slamming up against his own horse, which in turn began to dance about.

'How do we get out of this one?' Huffaker yelled. 'Come on, *Mister* Smartass, get us out!'

Lyedekker shoved the two loaded bags into Amabel's arms.

'You hang on to those, honey, like they were your best silk drawers!'

A second horse was hit. It went to its knees instantly, exposing Huffaker to the gunfire coming across the street. He snatched his rifle from its sheath and turned for the boardwalk. Missing his footing he sprawled full length on the boards. As he struggled to his feet a bullet clipped his left arm, drawing a lot of blood and an equal amount of swearing.

'Sam, let's go!' Lyedekker yelled.

'Go where?' Huffaker asked. He lurched upright, threw his rifle to his shoulder and triggered a round of shots that cleared the streets temporarily.

'We'll find somewhere to hole up, give us time to work something out,' Lyedekker said, as if his voicing

117

the thought solved all their problems.

Huffaker looked as though he was about to protest, so Lyedekker turned away. He took hold of Amabel's arm and began to drag her along the boardwalk. Out of the corner of his eye Lyedekker could see the cautious citizens of Paxton emerging from cover, and he knew damn well that getting out of this town was going to be one hell of a job.

A rifle opened up, bullets chewing splinters of wood from the boardwalk and the front of the building that Lyedekker was passing. Lyedekker began to run, crouching low, forcing Amabel to do the same.

'Sweet Jesus!' Huffaker yelled out. 'We got to get off the damn street!'

Lyedekker knew he was right. Sooner or later one of the outraged citizens was going to get a grip of himself, calm down, and do some straight shooting. And it would only take one well-placed bullet to do the trick. Lyedekker threw a swift glance along the street. A few yards along was a double-fronted general store, the door open.

'Sam, in there,' Lyedekker yelled. He dragged Amabel toward the store. Yet even as they drew level with the store a slight figure wearing a long apron stepped out through the door. Lyedekker got a swift impression of a thin, balding man, hefting a long-barrelled shotgun in his white hands. Startled eyes settled on Lyedekker's wild face, held for a moment, then the pursed lips opened in the birth of a shout, the shotgun lifting. Lyedekker swivelled the rifle in his hand, finger touching the trigger. The shock of the bullet, fired from less than a couple of feet, lifted the fragile figure and slammed him back against the door frame. The shotgun slipped from nerveless fingers as the man twisted forward in agony, the white apron suddenly wet with pulsing red. As the man crumpled to the boardwalk Lyedekker stepped over him, thrusting Amabel into the store before him. Huffaker followed them, kicking the door shut and slamming home the bolt.

For a long moment there was silence as they caught their breath. Lyedekker peered around the shaded interior of the store. They seemed to be alone. But he saw no profit in taking chances.

'Sam, take a look in back. You find anybody get rid of 'em. And make sure any doors and windows are shut and locked.'

Huffaker nodded and vanished amongst the stacked goods.

'This could turn out to be right cosy, honey,' Lyedekker grinned at Amabel. She regarded him coldly.

'I think you have walked into a trap you won't get out of so easily, Mr Lyedekker,' she said.

Lyedekker had crossed over to the counter. He broke a large wedge of cheese from a round and took a bite from it.

'I ain't dead yet, honey,' he said.

'You don't think those people out there are going to let you get away, do you?'

Lyedekker threw the cheese aside angrily.

'I don't give a damn about those bastards! They want me they're going to have to come and get me. And that'll cost 'em.'

'Does everybody have to pay for your actions, Mr Lyedekker? Isn't it about time you did some paying?'

Lyedekker stared at Amabel.

'Don't give me none of your fancy talk, honey, 'cause it ain't going to do you one bit of good.'

'Mr Lyedekker, I never thought it would,' Amabel replied. 'Not for a single moment.'

Huffaker returned from his inspection of the rear.

'All clear,' he said. 'No back door or windows,' he added. 'This place was built on the cheap.'

'Tight-assed storekeepers,' Lyedekker grumbled. 'All they want is profit.'

Amabel smiled. 'Well, there's something you have in common then.'

'Hugo, I don't like bein' a misery,' Huffaker said. 'But how in hell are we going to get out of this damn box?'

Lyedekker had crossed over to peer through the front window. Out on the street he could see armed men moving back and forth. They were positioning themselves behind every available piece of cover. As he watched them an odd feeling of contentment came over him. He'd always known that one day he would face a final confrontation. A showdown. A time when his violent ways would bring him face to face with a last-stand fight against those he hated. Anything and everything to do with law and order and orderliness. Lyedekker had been fighting those things ever since he could remember. Way back to when he'd been a raggedy-assed kid of twelve, on his own in an uncompromising world. Then he'd had to survive on his wits and by brute force, taking what he wanted, when he wanted, and caring little who got hurt during the taking as long as it wasn't himself. His way had followed him into adult life, and it had been easier to stay that way than try to change.

Not that he'd wanted to change. As far as he could see everybody took what they wanted when they wanted it. The only difference being that they had it all wrapped up so it looked legal and nice and civilized. Right now he was up against all those bastards. They were out there, armed to the teeth, ready to blow him from hell to breakfast given half a chance. Lyedekker grinned at his reflection in the glass of the store window. All right, boy, let 'em come! I'm ready for the sons of bitches! They might get me in the end, but by God, it'll be a fight to remember! One that'll go down in the history books. The day it took a whole damn town to kill Hugo Lyedekker!

'Hugo? You hear me?' Huffaker's voice cut through Lyedekker's moment of calm.

'Yeah. I hear you, Sam,' Lyedekker said. He turned away from the window and walked slowly across the floor.

Huffaker watched him, puzzled. Then he said: 'So what do we do?'

'Remember the Alamo,' Lyedekker said softly, almost to himself, as if he was alone in the store.

Huffaker stared after him as though Lyedekker had suddenly gone mad.

'Remember the what?' he asked. 'Goddam remember the goddam what?' he repeated, his voice rising to a wild bellow of frustration.

The front windows of the store exploded inwards, glass showering across the store. Bullets ripped their way through boxes and cans, tearing open sacks, spilling the contents on the floor. A bottle standing on the counter shattered, spraying pale liquid in the air.

Huffaker, picking himself up off the floor, inspected a ragged gash across the back of a hand. He absently wiped the blood off on his shirt, shaking his head slowly. When he looked across at Lyedekker there was a knowing gleam in his eyes.

'You bastard,' he said forcefully. 'You're going to enjoy every damn minute of this!'

Lyedekker was behind the counter. He had found boxes of ammunition on a shelf and he was reloading his rifle and handgun. He was wearing a wide grin and as he caught Huffaker's eye he began to laugh. The sound rose until it filled the store, floating out through the shattered windows and across the street to where the citizens of Paxton sat waiting. They heard the sound and they knew that they were in for one hell of a fight. They knew something else, too. They were facing more than just an outlaw with a ready gun. They were facing nothing less than a madman!

14

Paxton looked like an armed camp to Frank Angel as he rode in. There wasn't a woman or a child in sight, and every man he saw was armed. There was a tense, strained atmosphere hanging over the place too, strong enough to be noticed.

'Hey, you! Just hold it! And keep your hands in sight!'

Angel reined in and turned his head to glance at the speaker. He saw a big, hard-faced man approaching. The man was carrying a double-barrelled shotgun and he had the muzzles aimed directly at Angel.

'You talking to me?' Angel asked.

'I don't see anybody else around,' the man said. 'And don't give me any horse shit talk neither, friend, else I'll empty both barrels through you and say sorry later!'

Angel sighed wearily. He was tired, dirty, and sore, and he needed trouble like he needed a third leg.

'You want to start again,' he suggested. 'Just tell

me what I've done wrong and we'll sort it out.'

The man spat in the dust. 'What you doing in Paxton?'

'Maybe I'm passing through. Maybe I came to see my grandaddy. An' maybe I came to rob the goddam bank.'

The man's reaction to Angel's last remark was instantaneous and violent. He lunged forward, lifting the shotgun, and Angel knew with a mounting shock that the man was going to fire. He kicked his feet free from the stirrups, letting his body roll from the saddle, to the left of and beneath the rising gun-barrells. Clearing his saddle Angel let himself drop to the ground. He heard the flat boom of the shotgun, caught the following angry curse coming from the man. Then he was hitting the ground, his shoulder taking the impact as he rolled, came to his feet and unwound his long frame in a single movement. Angel's right fist followed through, sledging into the man's exposed stomach, drawing a deep grunt of pain. The man doubled over, the shotgun sagging, and a careless finger tripped the second trigger. The blast from the shot tore a raw crater in the hard earth, spitting up sharp splinters. Angel was angry enough to hit the man again, clubbing him across the back of his thick neck, dropping him to the ground like a pole-axed steer.

'Now you just stand where you are!'

Angel's head came up. His face was taut, his eyes glittering with anger as he faced this new challenger.

He found himself face to face with a keen-eyed, fresh-faced youngster who couldn't have been more than twenty. The young man was slim, dark-haired, dressed in neat clothes. He held a cocked gun in his hand and wore a badge on his shirt that read Deputy Marshal.

'You figure I'm going to get any sense out of you?' Angel asked.

The deputy stepped forward. Behind him were a number of armed men.

'What's going on?'

Angel shrugged. 'All I know is I've just ridden in and got shot at.' He grinned suddenly. 'Hard on the nerves but it's an original way of saying hello.'

The deputy glanced at the man on the ground.

'I knew I'd done wrong letting Harry Knape look after this job.' He lowered his gun and glanced at Angel. 'Harry has a knack of upsetting folk. Though I suppose this time he's got good reason.'

'Am I allowed to hear it?'

'If you stay in town more than five minutes you'll find out,' the deputy said. 'Two days ago a couple of wanted men tried to hold up the bank. They killed the manager then made a run for it. The marshal tried to stop him but they gunned him down too. Before anyone could stop them they holed up in Zac Handy's store. Killed Zac when he tried to stop them. We've had 'em bottled up in there ever since but we can't get them out and they've shot three people in the meantime.'

'You know who they are?' Angel asked.

The deputy nodded. 'Yeah. We soon found out.'

'Hugo Lyedekker and Sam Huffaker?'

The deputy's eyes flickered across Angel's face.

'Just what do you know about 'em, mister?'

'Enough so we could stand here talking all day,' he said. 'Can we go to your office?'

The deputy nodded. He beckoned to a man standing nearby. 'Jim, take this man's horse to the livery and see it's looked after.' To Angel: 'The office is down this way, mister . . . ?'

'Frank Angel's the name.'

The deputy nodded. 'I'm Linc Culhane. The marshal was my father.'

'Hell of a way to take over a job.'

Linc turned his face away for a moment and Angel didn't intrude. After a moment Linc said:

'My father had kept this town clean for a long time. He was well liked. Killing him was the worst thing those bastards could have done. Every man who can carry a gun is on the street. Won't matter if it takes a year. We'll wait.'

'What about the girl who was with them?' Angel asked.

'She's in the store.' Linc's face was grim. 'She'll get the same treatment.'

Angel stopped in mid-stride, grabbing hold of Linc's arm. He spun the young man round.

'You just back off there, boy, and get your facts right! That girl is with them because she's a hostage:

127

She hasn't any choice, so you get that through your head!'

'You know that for sure?'

'Damn right I do. I've been trailing Lyedekker for days trying to get that girl away from him!'

They reached the jail and Linc led the way inside. He closed the door and motioned Angel to sit down.

'You look like you've had a hard ride, Mr Angel. Want a cup of coffee?'

Angel sank into a chair. He took the hot mug of coffee from Linc and watched the young man sit self-consciously behind the desk where no doubt his father had previously sat.

'Can't help but feel I shouldn't be sitting here,' Linc said. 'It's like I got the job without earning it.'

'Sometimes it happens that way,' Angel said, reminding himself of how he had stepped into the position of top investigator after the death of the Department's best man. The difference was that in Angel's case, he himself had brought about the man's death.

It seemed an eternity ago, as he remembered that desperate fight in the darkness, beside the railroad tracks just outside Trinidad: the kill-or-be-killed struggle between two expertly trained combatants. And Angel had almost died that night. Might have if he'd let his feelings for the other man weaken him. But they had trained him too well; had hammered survival into him so deep that it was against his instinct to even think about quitting. And in the end he had killed the man he'd once thought of as a friend. The way things had turned out it couldn't have ended any other way. But it still hurt to recall that night. It still hadn't healed. The mental scar remained. Angel didn't think it ever would heal. And he thought, damn you Angus Wells for the legacy you left me, and in the same moment he added: and I'm still sorry it had to happen!

Angel sat upright, placing the steaming mug on the desk. He reached into his coat and drew out a thin oilskin and unwrapped it. He laid the folded sheet of parchment in front of Linc Culhane. A few moments later Angel's circular badge was placed beside the parchment.

Linc picked up the badge and studied it. Then he opened the parchment and read it, digesting it fully.

'You know what all that means?' Angel asked.

Linc smiled. 'One of the things means I'm demoted as long as you're in Paxton.'

'Not as bad as it sounds,' Angel said. 'Look, I'm after the same thing you are. To get Lyedekker and Huffaker out of harm's way. I ain't finicky how I do it. As long as no harm comes to that girl.'

'How did she get involved with Lyedekker in the first place?'

Angel picked up his mug. 'Fill that up again and I'll tell you.'

Over his second mug of coffee Angel told Linc Culhane the story. The young deputy sat back as Angel concluded, shaking his head in awe.

'Hell, man, you've gone through more in a few days than has happened in Paxton since the day I was born.'

Angel put down his empty mug. He stood up.

'From what I've seen out there you seem to be making up for that right now!'

As they made for the door Linc asked:

'Well, it's your game now, Mr Angel. What do you want to do?'

'Take a look at the store first. And the name's Frank.'

Linc nodded. 'Can we smoke 'em out?'

'Knowing Lyedekker he isn't going to come unless this town is evacuated. And even then he's liable to change his mind.' They were outside now, moving along the boardwalk to where the main group of armed men stood.

'That's the store,' Linc said, pointing to a building across the street.

'Back way in?' Angel asked.

Linc shook his head. 'No. Old Zac was a worrier. He was always scared somebody was going to rob him. When he had the store built he didn't have a back door put in. Or back windows. Just the front door and the two front windows. It's the only way in and the only way out. For them and us.'

They reached the grouped men. Hostile stares were thrown in Angel's direction but he ignored them.

'Linc, who is this feller?' somebody asked.

130

'All you boys need to know is that he's in charge of the situation from now on. I take my orders from him and so do you.'

'The hell you say!'

'Son of a bitch can't just ride in and tell us what to do!'

'Damn right!'

'Maybe we ought to run him out of town!'

'This is our business, mister, so stay out of it!

Angel let them all have their say, and when there was a temporary lull in the conversation he said:

'You men had better listen because I'm only going to say this once. I don't give a damn what you figure is right and wrong here. My job is to deal with Lyedekker and Huffaker. I've got the authority to do it and if need be I can even bring in the Army to establish law and order. If anybody wants to argue with me, let him step out and we'll settle it. Then he can cool off in one of the cells back there. But I'm warning all of you. I don't want any vigilante-style justice. Lyedekker has a girl with him in there. She's a hostage. There against her will and Lyedekker will kill her if he has to.'

'Linc, you believe all this? For all we know he might be one of Lyedekker's men. Maybe this is just a trick to break those bastards out!'

'Yeah! How do we know this guy is who he says is!'

Linc Culhane raised his arms to silence the shout-ing.

'I know who he is. And what he's told you is correct.'

'Well maybe we don't take much stock in your word, boy!'

The man who had spoken thrust his way to the front of the group. It was the man Angel had tangled with on his arrival. The man Linc had named as Harry Knape. It was obvious that Knape resented Linc Culhane's power. He threw a murderous glance in Angel's direction, his beefy face darkening with anger.

'This is our town, boy. Our bank that was busted and our friends who got killed. You figure we're going to stand around while you play games? Just 'cause you figure you got a right to wear that badge!'

'I'd watch what I said, Harry,' Linc warned.

Knape laughed harshly. 'What you going to do, boy, put me in jail? You and your friend?'

'Harry, you're talking crazy!' Linc said. 'Now break this up . . . all of you . . . and let—'

'No!' Knape yelled. 'We've already decided the way we're going to handle it! And no son of a bitch lawman is telling me how to handle things!'

There was a murmur of assent from the other men. Angel saw that they were behind Knape. Before he could do anything Linc Culhane made a bad mistake. He took a step forward, his hand reaching for the gun holstered on his hip.

'Ease off, Linc . . .' Angel began, but it was too late. The angry murmur rose and the bunched men surged toward Linc and Angel.

'Get 'em out the way!' Harry Knape yelled. 'Toss 'em in the jail! Jack, you go get that blasting powder and we'll blow them bastards out of that store!'

Knape's words reached Angel with the impact of a bolt of lightning. The damn fools! What the hell did they think they were doing! Didn't they give a damn about Amabel? If they started messing around with explosives anything could happen. A cold wash of terror spread over him, and Angel went wild. He began to lash out at the men around him, unmindful of whom he hurt. He drove two men away, seeing their angry faces crumble into pained masks as his fists caught them.

But there were others to take their places and their anger swelled up and exploded in mindless violence. Angel and Linc Culhane were struck from all sides, overpowered by sheer physical numbers. Numb and bleeding they were driven across the boardwalk until they had their backs against the wail. Fists, boots, gun butts, all were used against them, and when they were unable to stand on their feet they were dragged off in the direction of the jail. . . .

Angel detached himself from the pain, the pulsing throb of agony that burned his battered body. He half-opened his eyes, blinking away the haze that was threatening to close them. He was being half-dragged half-walked along the boardwalk towards the jail. There was a man on either side of him, each holding one of his arms. Angel offered no resistance.

133

The time wasn't right. Not while the rest of the men could see. He was going to have to wait until they were inside the jail. Then he could make his move.

The man on Angel's right booted open the door to the jail. Angel was hauled into the office.

'Come on, Fred, get Linc in here,' a man's voice yelled. 'Let's get these two in a cell. I don't want to miss all the fun.'

'Hell, no, it'll be like the Fourth of July all over,' a second man laughed.

There was a muffled clatter of boots on the office floor. A man grunted with annoyance:

'This son of a bitch is damn heavy!' Then the office door banged shut.

And Frank Angel thought: Now!

His swung his arms up, curling them around a leg of each of the men holding him, then jabbed his heels hard against the floor and thrust upright. The two men were thrown off their feet, falling heavily to the floor, and before they had even touched ground Angel had spun round to face the remaining pair who were holding Linc Culhane. One of them reacted with reasonable swiftness and his fingers were actually touching the butt of his holstered gun when Angel hit him. The outer edge of Angel's right hand caught the man across the side of the neck. To an observer it would have looked like a casual, almost careless blow. But it was delivered with terrible force, placed accurately, and the man went down as though all his bones had dissolved.

Angel continued his move, following through with a bunched left fist that struck the other man on the point of his jaw. The sound of impact was solid, the force of the blow snapping the man's head back brutally, driving him back against the office door with a thump. The man slid sideways across the door, pitching to the floor.

As Angel turned about he saw that one of the men who had been holding him was coming slowly to his feet. The man had a glazed look in his eyes, yet he was clumsily fumbling for his holstered gun. Angel laid the toe of his boot across the side of the man's skull, whereupon the man lost all interest in what was going on around him. Bending over the fourth man, Angel took away his gun, then he dragged the man to his feet, shoving him against the wall.

'You move, feller, and I'll shoot your kneecaps off!' Angel warned.

The man took one look at Angel's battered, bloody face, the cold eyes, and knew that he had better do as he was damn well told.

'Linc? You all right?' Angel asked.

Linc Culhane stood up slowly, sleeving blood from a ragged gash over one eye. He touched his finger-tips to a swollen lip.

'Hard to tell,' he said. 'Do I look as bad as you?'

Angel smiled. 'Yeah!'

Linc winced visibly. 'Then God help me,' he muttered. He glanced around the jail. 'What happened here?'

135

'The boys and me came to an understanding,' Angel said. 'Linc, let's get them in the cells.'

Linc nodded. He pushed open a door and ushered the first man through. Angel caught hold of a pair of legs and began to drag one of the unconcious men across the floor. Minutes later all four men were locked up in one of the cells.

Back in the office Linc peered out of the barred window. 'Now what do we do?'

'Not we, Linc,' Angel corrected. 'You stay put. I'll handle it.'

'One, you're hurt. And two, there's a hell of a lot of them out there.' Linc came across to where Angel was checking his gun. 'Why risk it?'

'It's my job,' Angel said. 'And a lot of those men are your friends. They might not seem to be right now, but when this is over a lot of them are going to be sorry. It isn't going to bother me if I have to hurt any of them. But you stay out of it.'

Linc went and sat down behind the desk. He watched as Angel moved to the door. Easing the door open a little Angel found he could see along the street. The main group of men were still across the street from the store. They seemed to be waiting for something to happen.

'There a back way out of here, Linc?'

'Yeah. Far end of the cell block.'

Angel nodded. 'Keep both doors locked and don't open them for anyone except me.'

Linc bolted the office door, then followed Angel

through to the cell block. As Angel slipped out through the door, Linc asked:

'Frank, what are you going to do?'

Angel paused for a moment.

'Hell, Linc, I thought you were going tell me,' he said with a dry chuckle, and then he was gone.

15

If you don't have a definite plan of action, they used to drill into him at the Department, use your initiative. Improvise. Create something out of nothing. Make it up as you go along. We've given you the theory, you put it into practice. If nothing else works you can always pray for a miracle. As he moved swiftly and silently along the backlots of Paxton's business establishments, Angel would have settled for a dozen US Marines.

He came level with the rear of the building directly in line with the store where Lyedekker and Huffaker were holed up. He paused there, pressed hard up against the rough planking, desperately trying to figure out what he was going to do next. One thing was obvious. It was no damn good at all expecting any of the men on the street to listen to him. They'd worked themselves up to fever pitch, and nothing less than a hanging was going to cool them down.

Angel considered the facts. The mob, it appeared,

were going to use blasting powder in an attempt to blow a way into the store. Angel saw that his prime concern would be to stop that happening. A lot of people could get hurt in a hasty explosion, and he admitted that Amabel's safety was top of his list. Angel didn't particularly care whether Lyedekker or Huffaker got hurt. Nor was he too bothered about the bloodthirsty citizens of Paxton. They were grown men, aware of what they were doing, and if they blew themselves to hell Angel wasn't going to shed any tears. But if Amabel was harmed because of their stupidity Angel was going to be very upset.

He moved on along the line of buildings until he was further down the street, then cut down an alley. In the shadow of an overhanging veranda he was able to look along the street and see the whole scene.

There was the store, seemingly deserted, its front windows shattered. The body of the shot owner still lay where he'd fallen.

Across the street stood the bunched group of men, watching and waiting.

A little closer to Angel were some more men. They were clustered around a flatbed wagon, intent on some preparations. One man held a couple of saddled horses. Angel recognized Harry Knape's burly figure in amongst the group.

Angel took a quick glance along the street in the other direction. A single horse stood at a hitch rail no more than a few yards away from him. Apart from the animal the street was deserted.

A flurry of activity caught Angel's attention. The group around the wagon broke apart. Two of the men mounted the waiting horses, leaned over to receive bulky objects from the others. They were easily recognizable as small, wooden barrels, the type that held blasting-powder. Angel could see that each barrel had been placed in a rope sling, and that trailing fuses hung from the sealed bung-holes. A man stepped forward and struck a match. He raised the match and touched it to one fuse, then moved quickly to the second. As the fuses sputtered into life the two riders put spurs to their horses and set off along the street, angling in towards the store.

Angel stepped out from his cover, making for the horse at the hitch rail. He freed the reins and flung himself into the saddle, savagely dragging the horse's head round. He turned the horse up the street, pulling out his Colt, leaning forward across the animal's neck.

He knew now what they intended doing. As each man rode past the store he would swing his barrel in through the broken window. And when those barrels of powder went off they would lay waste the interior of the store. They would also do the same to anyone inside the store at the time.

Which meant Lyedekker.

And Huffaker.

And Amabel Rowe!

Angel slammed in his heels, sending his horse leaping forward. He thumbed back the hammer on his Colt, and laid it across the horse's neck, triggering a swift shot at the closer of the two riders. His shot missed by inches. Angel swore, cocked and fired again. The rider's horse screamed shrilly as Angel's bullet struck. Blood sprayed out in a pale mist. The horse shuddered and went down on its knees. The rider lost his grip on the reins and was pitched from the saddle. He hit the ground on his face, slithering helplessly in the dust. The barrel, with its glowing, spitting fuse, bounced from his hand and rolled along the street.

Behind Angel the men grouped around the wagon began to move up the street. They were shouting in his direction, but Angel chose to ignore them. He wanted the other rider. The man was almost level with the front of the store now, leaning over in his saddle as he started to swing his barrel.

Angel hauled in on the reins, sliding from the saddle before the horse had come to a halt. Swinging up his Colt, Angel held it two-handed. He braced himself, held his aim as he followed the target, then triggered two quick shots. He saw the rider jerk in his saddle, his body arching. Blood stained the sleeve of his shirt where Angel's bullets had hit. The hit man's fingers loosened their grip on the rope and the barrel of powder flew free, falling short of the store window. The wounded man had the presence of mind to turn his horse away from the store, cutting sharply across the empty street.

And then the first barrel of powder exploded. The

blast was heavy, sound reverberating along the street. Windows shattered, glass showering the air. Much of the damage was done by flying debris, though a lot of glass broke due to the shock of the blast. A ball of fire hung briefly over the hole caused by the explosion, then it faded, swallowed by a dense, billowing cloud of white smoke that began to drift across the street.

Aware of the second barrel of powder Angel moved on up the street. His ears rang from the shcok of the blast. Around him men were shouting, running back and forth, losing themselves in the swirling cloud of powdersmoke and dust. Somewhere a man was yelling, a pained, self-pitying sound.

Angel was suddenly confronted by a wild-eyed figure: a man covered in dust, blood streaking one side of his face. His lips peeled back in an angry snarl as he recognized Angel.

'You son of a bitch!' the man yelled. He had a rifle in his hands and he began to lift it. Angel didn't hesitate. He slammed the barrel of his Colt across the side of the man's head, laying him out on the ground.

That was when the second barrel went up. It was a much more powerful blast than the first. The shock waves rushed out to meet Angel, picking him up and putting him flat on his back in the middle of the street. At the same time the explosion ripped out the front of the store. The air was suddenly filled by chunks of flying timber, slivers of glass, a two-yard section of the boardwalk. The ball of flame created by the blast set fire to the dry timber of the store-front.

Angel stumbled to his feet, eyes stinging from the acrid smoke and dust. Burning debris rained down from the dark cloud hanging over the street. Throwing up a hand to shield his face Angel made for the store, ignoring the curling tongues of flame billowing out from the ruined frontage.

A figure lurched out of the smoke and flame, its clothing charred and torn. The face was badly burned down the left side, the hand on the same side of the body shredded and bloody.

Sam Huffaker was in great pain. He had been close to the front of the store when the second explosion had occured, and the concussion had lifted him off his feet, throwing him across the floor. He'd felt the sudden wave of heat pass over him and it had taken a few seconds for him to become aware that his clothing was almost burning. He had tried to wriggle away from the tremendous blast of flame, but he wasn't fast enough. The left side of his face had shrivelled and blistered, and all down his left side he could feel the pulsing surge of burnt flesh. Something had struck his left hand, pain exploding in a searing flash, and when he'd taken a look his hand resembled a piece of butchered meat. Even in the midst of the confusion that followed the explosion, and despite his injuries, Huffaker thought of nothing else but surviving. He had struggled to his feet, stumbling through the dust and smoke, the falling debris, the rising flames. He found he still had his gun clutched in his right hand. Without conscious effort he took himself over the pile of shattered timber, once the store's frontage, and out onto the boardwalk.

And there he came face to face with Angel.

Huffaker didn't know the name of the man. But he recognized him as the one who had showed up in Hope. The one who had freed the hostages. Huffaker remembered the face. He remembered the moment when Lyedekker had run the man down with his horse. They should have made sure the son of a bitch was dead. If they had things might have turned out differently. But the mistake had been made, and the whole damn deal had gone wrong. And now the bastard was here. . . .

The moment he saw Huffaker Angel recognized him. And he saw the gleam in Huffaker's eyes. Twisting to the left, Angel thrust his Colt out and up, finger easing back on the trigger. He saw Huffaker's gun move too, coming round easily and fast. The two shots merged, brief flickers of flame issuing from the muzzles. Angel's left knee hit the ground and he braced himself, triggering a second shot, then another. He saw Huffaker stiffen, step back. The blackened shirt blossomed bright blood. Angel fired again, saw the bullet strike Huffaker's chest, driving the man over on to his back. Huffaker sprawled across the boardwalk, his right hand drumming against the charred planks. His body arched in silent agony, mouth wide. A gout of blood rose in his throat, spilling over his blistered lips, and then he was still.

Angel climbed to his feet, fingers busy reloading the Colt. He stepped up on to the boardwalk and into the wreck of the store, looking for Hugo Lyedekker and Amabel Rowe.

16

The store was empty!

Angel covered the building from front to rear. In a corner of the storeroom at the back he discovered the place where Lyedekker had chopped a hole through the boards to the outside. He went through the ragged gap. In the dust at the rear of the building he picked up scuffed bootmarks left by two people. Lyedekker had cut off to the north, making for a range of low hills that rose in undulating slopes behind the town.

Angel turned away from Paxton and made for the hills. He ran at a steady pace, his gun in his hand, cocked and ready, because he knew that by now Lyedekker must be close to the end of his endurance: chased and hounded and cornered, now forced to run again. Even someone as hard as Lyedekker had a limit. Once reached, a dangerous man became even more of a threat. More so because he would lose all control, letting slip his natural caution, allowing unpredictable emotions to dictate

146

his actions. In a situation like that a man assumed almost animal-like qualities, and as such he presented an unknown quantity. There was no way of figuring the way a man like that might act.

Moving up the lower slopes Angel thought he saw figures up above him. He couldn't be sure. He kept moving, letting the tracks in the dust guide him. The slopes began to rise at a sharper angle, and now Angel found he was crossing timberland. He spotted tracks in the soft mud at the edge of a narrow stream. It proved Lyedekker's state of mind. He wasn't even bothering to conceal his tracks.

Angel followed the trail into the timber. Again he found abundant sign to follow. Broken twigs hung from the bushes growing in amongst the timber. The soft ground underfoot showed every footprint. Lyedekker seemed to have but a single thought. To cover as much distance as possible, regardless of the trail he left in his wake.

Ahead of Angel the timber thinned out, revealing a sudden steep rise in the slopes. The trees gave way to rock and grass, and further on an even steeper, bare slope. Easing out of the trees Angel again picked up the trail and ran on. . . .

The single shot rapped out sharply!

It registered on Angel's mind and he went slack and dropped to the ground. The bullet whacked a rock to the left of him, leaving a white scar on the hard surface before it howled off into the air. Angel twisted round, his eyes searching the slope back from where he was lying. He caught a fragmentary glimpse of drifting powdersmoke, and saw too the figures standing on the slope above him. Angel brought up his Colt, finger easing back on the trigger as he held on his target. Then he lowered the gun, shaking his head. There was no way he was going to make a shot at this range. Not with Amabel standing beside Lyedekker.

A second shot came from Lyedekker. It was closer this time, sharp splinters of stone leaping up into Angel's face. Angel figured he was just as much at risk on the ground as he might be on his feet, so he gathered his legs beneath him, rose to a crouch and began to close the gap.

He saw Lyedekker lift his gun again, then hesitate. And then Lyedekker yanked Amabel Rowe's motionless figure closer to him and turned off up the slope.

Angel reached a level part of the slope. He raised his Colt and fired a warning shot, the bullet striking the ground yards ahead of Lyedekker. The outlaw faltered, then half-turned, his gun coming round and he fired hastily. The bullet went wide. In the same moment of time Amabel jerked free from Lyedekker's grasp, throwing herself to the ground. Lyedekker, exposed, triggered a wild shot in Angel's direction, then dropped to his knees beside Amabel. He placed the muzzle of his gun against the side of her head.

'You want her dead, mister, then just keep pointing that gun at me!' he yelled.

Angel fought back the rising panic. He knew that Lyedekker was capable of carrying out such a threat, and with Amabel at risk Angel wasn't going to aggravate the situation. He eased the Colt's hammer down and tossed the gun on the ground in front of him.

Hugo Lyedekker grinned, eyes blazing with excitement. He caught hold of the back of Amabel's dress, forcing her to stand, still keeping his gun against her head.

'You,' he called to Angel, 'I want up here! And fast!'

Angel made his way up the slope. He could feel Lyedekker's eyes on him the whole time. When he was within a few yards Lyedekker made an impatient gesture with his head.

'That'll do!'

Angel felt Amabel's eyes on him now. He glanced at her and caught the faint smile on her bruised lips. Cold anger rose in him as he saw what Lyedekker had done to her, and Angel had to force himself to keep from expressing his rage.

'I made a mistake not killing you back in Hope,' Lyedekker said. 'But I'll make up for it now!'

Angel didn't speak, and he saw the frustrated anger in Lyedekker's eyes.

'You son of a bitch,' Lyedekker snarled. 'I had a damn good thing going for me and you bust it wide open. I could have been a free man and a rich one if it hadn't been for you!'

'Do you really think Washington was going to pay you?'

'Damn right I do!' Lyedekker leaned forward. 'That else could they have done? With all those bigshots I was holding?'

'Washington doesn't play that game, Lyedekker,' Angel said. 'If they paid out every time some cheap crook tried it on it would be a full-time job.'

'You're a real smartass, ain't you? Got all the goddam answers!' Lyedekker swung the heavy Colt away from Amabel and trained it on Angel. Which was what Angel had been waiting for. 'What's your answer to this? *Mister* Smartass!'

Angel's answer was to step to one side, going down on one knee, in a swift, fluid motion that caught Lyedekker cold. As Angel's left knee touched the ground his right hand was already slipping free the Soligen steel throwing-knife concealed in the top of his boot. Angel flipped his arm back, then forward, the steel blade gleaming as it whickered through the air. The gun in Lyedekker's hand went off with a solid blast of sound. He'd jerked his body round in an attempt to regain his aim, pulling the trigger too quickly. The bullet skinned the top of Angel's right shoulder. Then the blade of the knife pierced Lyedekker's gun arm, high up, cutting into the hard muscle. Lyedekker gave a grunt of pain. He jerked the knife free, tossed it aside and tried to force his numb fingers to respond. Before he could cock the gun again Angel rose from his place on the ground, his hard body smashing into Lyedekker's, forcing the outlaw back. Lyedekker felt his gun fly from his hand. He had no time to worry over it because after that he was fighting for his life.

Feeling Lyedekker drop back Angel set himself, swinging a heavy right that caught the man full in the mouth, crushing Lyedekker's lips. Blood spurted from Lyedekker's mouth. Angel hit him again, a left to the stomach, then another right that clouted Lyedekker on the side of his jaw. The outlaw twisted half-round, leaving his body exposed. Angel sledged a crippling blow in under Lyedekker's ribs, drawing a high scream of pain from the man. Lyedekker's knees gave and he sagged to the ground. Angel caught hold of Lyedekker's tangled hair, dragging his head back. He drove his fist into Lyedekker's face, over and over again, until Lyedekker wore a bloody, broken mask. There was no mercy in Angel's face. No pity in his cold eyes, and he would have kept on hitting Lyedekker if a slim hand hadn't touched his shoulder.

'Please, Frank. That's enough. He's had enough.'

The wild rage left him. Angel turned and stared at Amabel Rowe, and right at that moment he'd never seen her looking so beautiful.

'Hello, Amabel,' he said for want of a better greeting.

'I knew you'd come.' She smiled.

'Amabel, this is getting to be a habit! Last time I had to go chasing all the way down into Mexico! I think you'd better stay away from trains. Unless I'm there to keep my eye on you!'

'Whatever you say, Frank.' Amabel reached out and took his hand, gripping his strong fingers, and it made her feel safe again.

'I'd better get you back to town. See if there's a doctor.'

Amabel put her arms around him, pressing close to him.

'I'm all right, Frank. Now I'm all right.'

'You're still going to be looked at,' Angel said. 'The Old Man'll skin me and hang me out to dry if he finds out I haven't treated you according to the book.'

'He's all right? Safe?'

Angel grinned. 'Hell, yes, woman! You'd think you were married to him! He's probably somewhere right now chewing holes in the carpet because he hasn't heard from me!'

Angel picked up Lyedekker's gun. He retrieved his knife and his own Colt. Bending over Lyedekker he removed the man's belt and used it to bind Lyedekker's hands behind his back. Then he hauled Lyedekker to his feet and prodded him down the slope.

As they made their way back down towards Paxton, Amabel said:

'From what I've heard, Frank Angel, you don't always play according to the book.'

He looked at her and saw that the old sparkle was showing in her eyes. He smiled.

'Let's say I sometimes read between the lines.'

'If I remember rightly,' Amabel corrected, 'you have a habit of writing your own rules.'

'Any complaints?'

Amabel shook her head. 'No. Just a thought that we might write a few more for ourselves!'

17

'You're looking better, Frank,' the Attorney-General said. 'Sit down.'

The Attorney-General settled himself in his own chair. He reached for and lit one of his infamous cigars. He drew deeply, sending thick clouds of smoke up towards the ceiling.

'How's the stomach?'

Angel was trying not to think about his stomach. He'd had the bullet taken out as soon as he'd arrived in Washington. The bullet was gone, but in its place was a neat incision, stitched up, and that was giving him more problems than the original wound.

'It's fine, sir.'

'Good.' The Attorney-General leaned forward. 'I've read your final report. I wish you'd cut down a little on the descriptive passages, Frank. It was like reading through the damn Bible. Be precise and brief.'

'Yes, sir.'

'Damn nuisance that trouble you had with those bounty hunters.'

'I thought that at the time, sir,' Angel said lightly.

The Attorney-General snatched the cigar from his mouth.

'One thing I can do without are your whimsical remarks.'

'Sir.'

'By the way, the Department has received a rather stiff letter from the railroad people. Apparently your little jaunt across country didn't do their locomotive much good. They say that it's burned out. Completely useless. The cost of repairing it seems to be prohibitive.'

'They're not suggesting the Department pays for the damn thing?'

The Attorney-General smiled. 'That's a good thought, Frank. We could deduct so much a month from your money.'

'Send the bill to the President. It was his say-so that got the train.'

'By the way, the President asked me to tell you well done.'

'Thank you, sir.'

'He's under the delusion that I am endowed with great confidence concerning you.'

Perish the thought! Angel mouthed silently.

'Lyedekker and Dagget will be tried at Yuma County Court in ten days. I have no doubt that this time they'll hang.' The Attorney-General smiled at some inner thought. 'By the time I'm through some-one is going to feel extremely sorry. Putting Lyedekker and his whole gang together in Yuma was a monumental blunder. It will have to serve as a lesson for the future.'

'We paid high for this lesson,' Angel said.

The Attorney-General nodded. 'In more ways than one.' He picked up a paper from the pile in front of him. 'The marshal of Paxton – Linc Culhane – has written. He regrets what happened there and says he can only apologize for the actions of certain persons.'

'It could have been worse,' Angel said. 'I'm glad I got there before the situation got completely out of hand.'

The Attorney-General sat back, watching Angel for a time.

'Under the circumstances, and taking into account all that had happened, plus your unavoid-able personal involvement . . .' There was a pause, 'and knowing your feelings . . . why did you bring Lyedekker in alive?'

Angel caught himself before he smiled. He'd been expecting the question for days, and he wondered why it had taken the Old Man so long to get around to it.

'It would have been easy,' he said. 'If Amabel hadn't been there I think I would have killed him.' Angel frowned, troubled. 'I'm not sure whether I was doing it for her or myself.'

The Attorney-General allowed a faintly mocking smile to edge his lips.

'That, my boy, is the influence a woman has over a man. It gets us all sooner or later. We get so we don't know left from right. Up or down.' The Old Man paused. 'But it shouldn't bother you too much, Frank. I mean, you're not all that involved with Amabel. Are you?'

Angel glanced across the desk, unsure how to take the Old Man's query. The Attorney-General's face was set, his expression stolid, but Angel was damn sure he'd detected a devilish gleam in the Old Man's eyes.

'So,' the Attorney-General said abruptly, veering off the subject. 'The doctor tells me you should be fit for duty in a week or so. Make it a week if you can. It's incredible how things pile up. There are a number of matters I'd like you to look into. But we can leave them until you come back.'

'Yes, sir,' Angel said.

The Attorney-General beamed across the desk. 'So you'll be off now?'

'Sir?'

'Places to go. Things to do.'

Angel got up and made for the door.

'Frank! Give her my best wishes, and tell her I'll be along to see her again sometime tomorrow!'

'I'll do that, sir,' Angel said without looking round. He was grinning all over his face as he made his way out of the building. There was no way of hiding anything from the Old Man. He'd known all along that Angel had been visiting Amabel every single day, spending every possible hour he could with her at the nursing-home where she was resting. By the time he reached the street the grin had changed to a laugh. A lot of curious stares followed Angel as he walked along Pennsylvania Avenue. He didn't notice a single one of them. His mind was on a tall young woman with honey-coloured hair and blue eyes. A woman who had the ability to make him feel good by just being there. She didn't need to speak, she didn't need to move. Her presence was the catalyst. Not that she was incapable of speech or movement. Far from it. She had a delightful voice, and the way she moved her supple body was unforgettable.

Angel didn't give a hoot about the Old Man's remarks. Maybe he was under some kind of influence. Maybe Amabel had got to him more than he might admit to. But so what? He was a grown man and no fool. He knew his own mind. Or did he? The thought presented itself unbidden. Angel brushed it aside. Of course he knew what he was doing. What did the Old Man think? That he was crazy? Angel started laughing again. That might be it, he thought. Maybe I am crazy!

He was still chuckling about it when he reached the nursing-home. Amabel was sitting out on one of the wide green lawns, drowsing in the warm sunshine, but she opened her eyes as he approached, smiling at him. She held out a slim hand, grasping his eagerly.

'Hello, Frank,' she said, and Angel knew without a doubt that nothing else mattered. They could all go to hell as long as he and Amabel could be together. Even if it was only for a short time. Until he was well enough to take his next assignment and she found herself behind her desk again.

For Frank Angel that was more than enough.